WHERE TALES GRIP

Your Imagination...Captured

Anthology of Award-winning Short Stories

ISBN: 978-1-7349744-0-9

Scribes Valley Publishing Company
Knoxville, Tennessee
www.scribesvalley.com

DEDICATION

This anthology is dedicated to those
whose imaginations are easily captured

To the authors featured in this book: Scribes Valley thanks you for
your time, patience, trust, and talent.

Take the path to the reading place

Escape your world, slow the pace

Lose yourself, take a mind trip

Beyond the norm, where tales grip

CONTENTS

GET GRIPPED
A Foreword by David L. Repsher, editor

Flash back with me.

Flash back to your youth, where you are holding open your favorite book. To the world, you are simply gazing at the pages, your eyes moving back and forth. To you, the words disappear as your captured imagination transforms them into a mental film with special effects shaper and more elaborate than anything you can witness on any screen. You are gone, transported by your imagination out of your body and out of your surroundings.

Ah, the power and wonder of a captured imagination! To have your imagination, inconceivable in size and strength, focused on a story that you become part of, a willing participant in events and locations that would not be possible in the real world.

And now some questions. Are you still able to do it? As an adult, can your imagination still be captured as easily as when you were young? Or have you fallen into a classic mind trap? How many times in your life were you told "you need to grow up?" *Ouch!* Five words that are like Kryptonite to an imagination. People who use those words, while *possibly* meaning well, don't know the harm they may be causing. Unfortunately, many take those words to heart and let their imaginations sit in a dark corner, used rarely, if at all. How sad!

Quick! Turn the page and get gripped in the great stories featured in this anthology. Prove to yourself that you've still got an imagination worthy of being captured. Become a role model for those with a squelched imagination.

And most of all: Enjoy yourself!

FIRST PLACE

THE RIDE

©2020 by JoDean Nicolette

Behind him, morning arrives. The Sierra peaks, ragged as his breath, allow the sun to emerge and shine gray on his shoulders. He wraps his fingers in Maizy's mane, his wedding ring glinting through the tangled black hair. Two hundred riders mill around them, this side of the chalk line. A sea of white helmets, a roll and surge like diesel-stained foam on a wave, competitors faceless underneath—riders of one mind, but each alone in the fray. Excitement, fueled by nerves and caffeine, ripples as steel shoes strike the hardpack. The horses blow and snort, the steam from their nostrils churning the brittle mountain air. The red start banner sways, while rumps and bellies bump and jostle, and riders' thoughts ricochet quick as the bodies beneath them. One hundred miles of difficult race ahead: equipment, training, the trail. The persistent question: *Are they ready?* Amidst the tumult, this man and his horse are still.

His wife, at this moment, is lying with her eyes closed between the organic cotton, high-thread-count sheets of their bed, surrounded by her *Caribbean-cyan* teal walls, under shelves heavy with his brass trophies and winners' cups. The spoils gathering dust in this room—the haven they built together, a shelter for their dreams and their future. The early sun bounces off her Pilates ball in the corner and against the pill bottles on her bedside table. Too sick, she says yet again, to come to the race. Too fatigued to crew for him at the aid stations where other wives wait to offer water and food to the horses and riders passing through. The other wives lounge at Robinson Flat, mile thirty-six, in folding chairs under beach umbrellas and rolled out awnings. They're parked next to Igloo coolers, cold drinks in hand, making jokes about being married to the riders. *He tracks mud,* one says, waving her Diet Coke in the air, *Trails hay, smells of horse and horseshit.* Later in the day, after the crews have relocated to Foresthill Mill at mile seventy, they've escalated to horse widows, abandoned for the four-legged mistress, with longer manes, leaner haunches, simpler needs. *Gone more than he's home,* the next one says as she stirs the bucket with oats and apple-flavored electrolytes. *Training ride today, trot long and steady, need to work the hills. And Saturday. And Thursday. And the week before.*

Or maybe his wife's eyes are not closed. Maybe they're open as the light slants through the Brazilian-teak Levelors, watching the muscles in *his* chest as he holds himself above her, his fingers wrapped in her hair as he rides, as she moves beneath, with a motion as natural as breathing.

The man's thighs tense and Maizy lurches forward. He jerks her back, harder on the bit than he means to be. He relaxes and exhales *Easy...*barely a sound. She flicks her ears in answer, and straightens, squaring herself on all four, supporting him without effort. The morning is chilled, but Maizy is warm, her heat rising through her rider. She looks where he looks. Straight ahead. West. Through her ears, he sees the night lingering in the mountains, the shadows draping the lodgepole pine, the western juniper, the granite. The course hides there. He believes if he looks hard enough, if his glare burns the first light into the trees and the canyons, then somehow the next hundred miles will shorten. He will draw the trail in, like a rope. The rocks and the dust will roll beneath them, the finish attainable, the final chalk line disappearing under Maizy's ringing hooves.

A woman on a bay gelding bumps against them, her blue

leggings whining against his thigh. *Sorry,* issues with steam from her mouth, and he smells the coffee she drank before mounting. The gelding swishes his tail and it stings his arm. Maizy pins her ears and snaps her teeth at his shoulder so that he twists his head away. The woman has bucked teeth and a brown pony tail and resembles her horse. Partners, maybe, who have grown together over time and miles, donning each other's mannerisms like some older couples do. A head tilt, twitched lip, shifted gaze. Perhaps she has a man who waits for her at Robinson Flat, leaning, scanning the trail, trying to catch a glimpse of her, willing her to be the first in. Her guy's still in it, despite the early mornings, and the days alone. The rider imagines him, with matted hair and crusty eyes, waking, hitching the rig, hauling hay, filling her thermos. And when she returns home, he's rubbing her neck and back, easing the fatigue and stiffness, letting her fall onto the couch without the words, questions, bids for attention.

The training, the preparation, the care, leave him spent. The race days are even more intense. Always sensing Maizy's condition—energy or fatigue, her symmetry of movement, her breath and pulse. After the last fifty miler, one of the countless practice runs for the Tevis, he had trudged from his truck to the house door, collapsed on the couch, still covered with salt, sweat, and muck—a kind of uniform, peeled away only with hot water and soap, and only when he musters the strength to rise and twist the knobs that would release the regenerating stream. The course followed him as he sank into the suede of the couch. Squeeze, rise, lean, balance. From next to him, his wife's fingers grazed his neck, and he leaned against her, relieved to be done scanning the trail, for obstacles, logs, turns. Finally, out of the saddle.

"How was the race?" she asked. Her breath felt warm on his neck.

"We won." His eyelids floated low. The fireplace, the photos over the mantle of their wedding, their trip to Catalina, Maizy's first place finish in last year's Big Horn 100, all grayed under his fatigue.

"I gathered that. Nice bowl. Silver. Who was there?" She straightened and he felt her lean forward, looking.

His eyes closed. "The usual. Cranes. Doug Wilson. Skeeter."

She squeezed his shoulders. "How was the course?"

"Good." he expelled the day with a long breath.

Her hands vanished and she stopped talking. His neck fell against the back of the sofa, his eyes, open now, rested on the ceiling. *Ecru*, she called the color. In the dimness, it's just plain white. "Fine. Really."

Silence. She scooted away. "I'd like to have someone put in raised beds for tomatoes this week. Would you like to plant anything else?"

"Up to you."

She sighed and heaved herself off the couch. Her feet slapped along the floor until she reached the kitchen. He knew she wanted to talk, but his thoughts kept circling back to the practice ride. Maizy charged out too fast for a fifty-miler, her focus on a gray mare twenty yards ahead. He had squeezed the reins, then pulled. Moved her sideways and back with his calves, the "jig-zag" he calls it, Maizy's forward drive interrupted by the lateral effort, which almost always works to call her back into him. When she finally gives in, when she lets him set the pace, that's when he lets her move forward uninterrupted. But that day, she was distracted the whole time, burning up energy against his leg and the bit. She powered over Coyote Peak, her shoes clanging against the stones and gravel, so he decided to let her go—the distance was short, half the Tevis—but then she had slipped on the descent. The replay assaulted him: Shale clattering beneath her front hooves, the sickening lurch forward onto her knees. He wasn't fast enough leaping off, so she bore his weight for the impact and then the launch back up. He should have dismounted and run beside her down into Leeds Valley, both to ease up on her and to watch her move, but Maizy never slowed. After a few off-beat steps she plunged forward, the blood on her knees tapping some ancient instinct to quash that gray ahead, along with the course. They'd blown across the line first, and Maizy's pulse dropped to sixty in four minutes, eclipsing the fitness criteria. Then she miraculously trotted out sound in front of the veterinarian who glared at her bloodied knees, and then at him, the woman shaking her head. Hours later, accepting the purse and bowl, running his thumbs along the engraving, he was still asking himself, had he done the right thing? Or had he injured her today in a way that would leave him without his partner tomorrow?

The official's clock blinks red. 5:05 AM. Ten minutes before the gun. He watches the seconds. Back at home, the numbers on the bedside clock are blue, like ice. 5:06, 5:07. He pictures her rolling over, turning her head, turning back, staring at the ceiling with her own burning glare. Considering *her* life. He's long gone, again. Already dressed, hitched, loaded, and off to a faraway trail, racing the rising sun. Does she think of him in the raw air, as she sinks deeper under the down? Does she picture his eyes as he strains at the trail ahead, shoulders hunched against the cold, lips dry and pursed, hands veined with dirt, tightening and relaxing against the reins? Does she root for him to win, or at least return home safe? Or does she imagine him, riding the long hours in the dark, clotheslined off Maizy by a branch or hurtled down a cragged slope, layered with centuries of lime and sediment and the pulverized bones of ancient creatures who had traveled the forbidding terrain too swiftly or with brazen abandon?

More likely, it's just another lonely morning as she reaches over, feels his dent in the mattress, long since cooled. Her hand rests for a moment before the first finger taps, softly, then harder as her fist slams against the sheet, and hauls herself up to face the day.

She calls him Wild Bill. As in Hickok, which used to be funny, when she'd bounce into bed wearing only his silver-belly Diamante Stetson. Back then, she was a bucking bronc herself, giving this cowboy the ride of his life. But now, when she calls him that, it's a stab, as though he's yay-hooing around the wild west, six-shooter in hand on his trusty stud Buckshot. No longer seeing him for who he is—an athlete, with his own skill set, riding for the purse, the sponsors, competing for the endorsements. For their high-thread-count sheets, their Levolor Blinds, their home. Their life.

The breeze lifts Maizy's forelock and she tilts her nose, flaring nostrils as if to smell the course ahead. She trembles and he know she yearns for battle. Her Hamdani Arabian blood is ancient, and with it comes the hunger to move, to command the earth and the sand. Bred for thousands of years in a place less hospitable than even these California mountains, these dusty, rugged Sierra Nevada miles from Auburn to Truckee.

Maizy is short for *Malika al kir-Mahboub*, or My Beloved Queen. And queen she is, not just by breeding. No, she understands what it means to be cherished. To be loved. Only the richest, softest leather for tack—bridle and saddle alive against her skin. Lightest titanium bit. Freshest grass, shipped from the loamy soils of Montana, each flake breaking sweetly between his fingers, releasing a scent that calls her to him, even if he has been away for days.

But winning is more than her power between his legs. Going the distance is a commitment to the thing itself—the day-to-day of it, the treks without the thrill. The miles of conditioning. Hours of rising trot, rocking with her shoulder, first one, then the other. Short stride, extended stride, it's an ultramarathon on his quads. Balls chafed into tenderized beef. Ass? One massive callous. After a ride, his knees ache and creak like unoiled pistons. He walks the stiffness from his back before he can cool Maizy down. It pays off though, all those miles. So, he *can* let her go when she asks it, those times with another horse in sight and she extending her trot to chug past, ears pinned, and nose out, content to let their competitors cough in the dust. It's in those moments that he senses her thrill, the other horses and riders consigned to the rear, and an open trail that shows clear as day before them. It's worth it when Maizy finishes the long runs and passes the vet's fitness check, and the judge slides the medal over his head at the podium, under the sun and the clarion morning sky.

He remembers her at the counter, the curve of her dark hair as it rests on her shoulder. It hides her face as she looks down into the display. The fluorescent lights light up the case, her flushed face, and the gold and glitter—stuff of luxury. And of winners. Of one more purse. She traces her finger along the glass before the salesgirl slides the cabinet open, lifts the shimmering strand. The diamond one. Tiffany. Five stones set in eighteen-karat gold. It's called "The Journey," which she's told him at least a thousand times. Young hands reach across the counter, slide the piece over her neck. Then the hands distort, the knuckles swell and he sees the grimeless, manicured nails. *His* hands. Acid rises from the rider's empty gut and he shakes the image away, stares forward into the darkness again. If he and Maizy can pull this purse, he can buy the necklace on the way home. It stings, the cost of it, how it has seemed out of reach for so long. But between his winnings and the stipends from gear companies and saddle makers, he'll pull the rig right up to the store's loading zone, trot in and grab it. He'll fasten the clasp himself, let The Journey land on her olive skin, where the diamonds will rest against her heart.

The clock blinks 5:12 AM. The chestnut in front of him lifts his left hoof, sets it down, lifts it again. His tail whips, his ears flatten. He's going to cow kick the bay mare next to him and the riders are clueless. They're too wrapped up in their own nerves to sense what's happening beneath them. Too fast, it's over. The chestnut humped its back, the shoe flashed, the bay mare stumbled sideways. Her mount almost comes off, then flies off on her own, hitting the gravel with two feet, but already leaning to look at the left hind. Her eyes close and her lips purse; tears shine through her lashes. The mare is bleeding at the hock, unwilling to set weight on the leg. They're out of the race. And he can see from the tension in the woman's shoulders, the tremble starting in her hands, that she's worried it might be worse than a scratched start. He pushes the possibility away— the empty trailer rattling home behind her. He closes his own eyes and rubs Maizy's withers, takes inventory of their bodies, relaxes his knees, feels her cocked hip. Her attention beneath him is subtle—a flick of the ear, a tenseness in the back, a ripple in the neck. Some riders never feel it. They go through the motions, get the technical aspects of walk-trot-canter, but nothing that requires that special sense in which horse and rider *know* each other. He can *feel* what Maizy's got and what she's got left. How steady her hooves take the slopes and the rocks, slide the steep gravel, pound the fast-packed forest roads. He knows when to notch her down, or gait up. It's all between his legs: her pulse, her breath. And in his seat: the power in her hind end. Some days Maizy's wound up, on the brink, ready to let loose as soon as he gives the signal. Other times she's off. Sore. Or spent. With nothing left for even one more step. On those days, he backs off, lets her hang with an extra flake of alfalfa. Instead, he checks the trailer, the bearings in the wheel wells, greases the hitch. Then he might clean the stall waterer, drop extra bedding on the floor. When she's figured out that he doesn't want anything from her, she comes to him with a nicker, and a nudge against his shoulder. A warm nuzzle on his ear.

And then there's her moods. She *is* a mare after all, stand-offish, and downright ornery at times, pinning her ears, and turning her hind end. That takes patience, and sometimes a smart crack with the lead rope's leather tag, just to reinforce who's in charge. But most of the time she's with him, moving with a turn of his head, or the slightest shift of his seat bones, understanding what he wants or needs before he thinks it. And when she's not, when she's focused on something else, some rustling from the brush next to the trail, or danger lurking on the horizon, he knows that, too.

He probably works in an office. Each day a routine. *His* eyes open to the soft chime of the alarm in the predawn light, the first sputter of coffee at 6:45. He yawns, stretches, mumbles good morning. Tie straightened at 8:17, collar buttoned down. Peck on the cheek at 8:22. Out the door to the tall brick and mortar, which stands steady at the corner of Stable and Boring. Where he rides the market, and the mutual funds, holding flash drives with his manicured hands, marred only by paper cuts. The hardest thing he does is balance a spreadsheet, and budget a beach vacation for the dark, rainy months. Does she admire this about him? This steadiness that she imagines will bring him home each night, headlights on the drive at 6:12, opening the door at 6:14, setting his briefcase down just inside the door. Ten o'clock news. In bed 11:07, with his arm around her waist, knees behind hers. And she smiles, the rider can see it, remembers it, her pale lips parting, the smallest overlap of her front teeth, the way they tug on her bottom lip. From when he was there, when she was proud of what he is, how he made her feel protected. Surrounded. Loved.

The race official climbs the wheeled platform in his orange and yellow vest. Bullhorn in hand, he describes the course, the technical miles. Twelve aid stations, six veterinarian checks. *Six!* Christ, they care more about the horses than the people. Just when they're rolling, a vet station looms, un-bit, un-saddle, all so Maizy's pulse drops to the cut-off in the designated time. The vets poke and prod, check hydration by lifting her lips and tugging at her skin. Trot in, trot out, to make sure she is sound. As if he can't tell when she's dry and exhausted. Two of the vet checks are mandatory one-hour holds, where the horses are supposed to eat and drink. The riders sleep. But that never happens, they just pace, both of them chomping at the bit. They wait for the signal. The check on the clip board, the nod of the head, waved hand, telling them what they already know: She's good to go.

All-totaled, there will be twenty thousand feet of elevation change, trails teetering on cliffs where horses and riders tread that brutal line between speed, condition, and fatigue. From the platform, the official scans the horses. *You'll be exhausted, dirty, parched, but if you push on, finish in under the twenty-four-hour time check, you'll have completed the toughest endurance run in the world.* The man's speaking to all of them, but for the rider, there's more than that. If he wins, crosses that line first after a grueling century of miles, he's convinced she'll believe they can do this. They can go the distance.

He thinks of another morning the sun was slow to rise. A morning when the cool was welcome, before the heat moistened their skin and robbed excitement for the ride. She was with him, preparing for his drive, wearing the deerskin gloves, a birthday gift. He walked the rig, checking the wheel lugs, the window latches, the tires, grease on the ball, brake lights. Her grunts and sighs reached around the trailer as she packed the truck bed. She hauled the water buckets, the tack box, dragged the wheelbarrow. He hung the hay bag and jogged up to help her. She had already drifted away.

"Hey, where'd you go?"

"Finished," she called from around the corner. She held the light from her cell phone over the flowers, plucking the deadheads off petunias, and pulling the locoweed sprouts from the mega-horseshit-fertilized dirt.

"Wow, thanks!" he said, reaching to close the tack door and loading the cooler into the cab. In the bed, the water buckets sat too high, where they might blow off, but that was fixable. He tugged her sleeve. She leaned in for a peck on her cheek, still studying the garden.

"Drive safe," she said to the crocuses.

As he turned, he saw the bale of alfalfa in the doorway of the hay shed. The sack of oat bran on top. Panic, and then annoyance. "You forgot Maizy's food!"

She glanced over. "Oh, sorry." But then looked away, shining the light into the dimness, something on the Harkness roses having caught her attention. "I left the check list on the counter."

He watched her pull off the gloves, lean and squint at the rose bushes. He turned away, launched the feed into the truck bed, climbed in and slammed the door. Hands on the wheel he searched his mind for a way to help her remember the alfalfa, remember the loading order that makes set-up and take-down smoother, help her remember the most essential things. Remember that she once loved him.

Out there, in the dark, there's so much beyond his control. Stuff that makes his training, his planning—all that he wants—completely irrelevant. The terrain is never what he thinks. Trees down. Loose rocks that roll under Maizy's hooves. Other riders crowding the course. Slurry from the unpredictable rains that can carry him down to places he never planned to go. Sometimes the numbers and the miles and the heartrates seem irrelevant, and he knows he can go the distance because they are partners and they are connected and it's easy and it just feels right. The wind lifts the hair off her face and she's moving underneath him like it's the most natural thing in the world. And then some stupid-ass vet pulls her from the race for an imperceptible lameness at the mandatory fifty-mile check, and his wife is shacked up with some deadbeat who has time to lay around in the morning and who helps himself to the aged Don Julio Añejo Tequila tucked under the hutch in the den.

At 5:14 he hears quiet. He knows the other horses are still there, the officials, the clock, the wind patrolling among the horses' legs as they stand on the flat. On one thousand pounds of courage, he sits staring ahead to where the clearing funnels into road, then again to a narrow dirt track and finally disappears into the wildest land known on this coast. The way ahead drops off the edge toward Squaw Valley, and he will have only Maizy's legs and heart and his judgment to carry them through. Under layers of clothing, doubt crawls up his spine like a tick. Has he done enough? Or too much? Can they really do this? When the official blows the thirty-second warning whistle, he hears none of it. Not the steel striking earth, the snorts, the prayers, the exhales as the other riders contemplate the dust and fatigue ahead. He does not hear the creak of saddle leather or the whisper of reins against Maizy's neck. He does not hear the starter's pistol as it shatters the mountain air. There is only Maizy's whistle of breath, as she blows a whinny to the sky, rocking back, lifting him into the air, carrying them into the shadows on a course too dark for him to see.

About the author:

For years JoDean succumbed to the field of medicine. Still a physician and teacher, she has now dedicated herself to a career in writing. JoDean's work has appeared in such publications as *The Sun Magazine, Printers Row Journal, The Rappahannock Review*, and *Inscape*. She is a Pushcart nominee and has been awarded the Grand Prize for Prose in The Maine Review's Rocky Coast Contest. JoDean is working on two books. She currently lives in the Bitterroot Valley with her dogs and horses, and her extremely patient husband, Ben.

SECOND PLACE

OLD HAT
©2020 by Phillip Frey

Eddie's reflection sat across the room on the dark TV screen. The two Eddies gazed at each other for a while, Eddie then asking, "Will she, or won't she?" There was no point in waiting for an answer. He pressed the remote. The other Eddie disappeared in a burst of color. A movie had popped on.

Nearly eight o'clock he noticed, still filled with the hope she would call.

They had met at the restaurant where he bartended. Emily had come in to meet a date for dinner but he never showed. "Must've been awful for her," Eddie said to the movie, thinking you couldn't tell by the way she looked.

He had spoken with her across the bar whenever he was not busy. He had even gotten her to laugh a few times. When Emily paid the check, Eddie had asked for her number. She took his instead, asking which night he would be off.

Thursday, he had told her.

"That's a good night. Call you sometime after seven."

Must be around forty, he had judged at the time, with a pretty face that was maturing well. He was sixty-two, and worried now over the age difference. About a twenty-year spread. The difference might have scared her off.

He had to admit, though, that at his age he still had a trim figure, was in good physical shape and referred to by some as an attractive man. As for the age difference, he had known plenty of women who liked older men. Though for now he could only think of one.

Eyes flicking to the TV, he had no idea what the movie was about. He pulled out his phone and laid it on the sofa's side table. "Not that late," he said to the phone. "Still time."

But then at 8:22 a riptide of disappointment tried to pull him under. He fought it off with the little hope he had left. He watched the movie. He watched the clock. He watched the phone.

8:48 and Eddie was dragged to the bottom.

Whenever he felt like this, he would put a hat on. He never understood why. Or maybe he did in a hazy sort of way; something to do with his father.

The old Mexican sombrero. He'll wear that one, he decided. Straw's soft and it has a colorful band.

He had bought it decades ago down in Ensenada. "Gretchen," he exhaled. They had met just after she moved here from Germany. She was a blue-eyed blonde. Eddie's heart would pound at the sight of her. About a year later, it was his head that had begun to pound.

During their two weeks in Ensenada, Gretchen would not stop talking about Dusseldorf, her family and friends, what a good life she had had in Dusseldorf.

Eddie shifted on the sofa, looked to the ceiling and repeated what he had said to her: "If you miss it so much, why don't you go back?"

She did, two weeks after their Ensenada vacation. Gretchen wrote Eddie from Dusseldorf. He never answered.

At least he still had the Mexican hat to show for it, he told himself.

Eddie rose from the sofa, took a step and stopped. Something might be wrong with the phone. Emily might have tried to call. Eddie lifted the phone and pressed for a dial tone. He listened to it, thinking how strange it was that a sound could sound so empty.

At the hall closet now, he gazed at his hats. They were on a shelf in a single stack, crown over crown. The Alpine was on top, gray in color with a feather stuck in the band. It had been a present from his mother.

He never wore it, thinking it would make him look like a European tourist. He kept it on top to shield the other hats from dust.

Under it, the Panama. Cream color with a wide dark-blue band. Eddie would wear it on hot sunny days, not too often though. He feared people would think him eccentric.

Eddie asked himself why he had always worried about what others thought, only to find the answer lay too deep for him to dredge it up.

"John Robert Crawford," he said to the Panama. They had met while Eddie lived in New York, just before Eddie's mother died. They did not need any ties from the past to become friends; it was immediate.

When Eddie had left for California, Crawford followed. It was no secret Crawford's ex-wife was already there, and that he could not forget about her.

A few weeks after Eddie and Crawford had arrived in Los Angeles they were in Beverly Hills, gazing at hats in a shop window. They both liked the Panama, and they each bought one.

Six months later Eddie wore his to Crawford's funeral. He had been drunk. Drove his car into his ex-wife's living room. She and her new husband were not home at the time.

"Guess he didn't know that," Eddie said to the closet floor, and he wondered whatever happened to Crawford's Panama.

Eddie's eyes settled on the brim of the black fedora under the Panama. "New York," he said with a quick nod.

Eddie was living off Third Avenue, around the corner from the *Caliban*. That was where he had first seen it. Black felt with a black snakeskin band, the band a half-inch wide with a thin gold clasp on its left side. A drinker at the bar had had it on, his eyes in shadow under the wide brim. Eddie complimented him on it and asked where he had gotten it.

"Italian hat-maker," the drinker said. "Where King Street meets McDougal."

Eddie went there the next morning and was measured for the fedora. Three days later he was back in the shop. He gave the domed crown a push downward, formed it and pinched the front. He put it on and curled the brim down over his left eye.

"You don't need a mirror to put it on," the hatter stated.

"My father taught me how." It was then that Eddie turned to the mirror. "Wish he were alive to see me in this one. It's perfect." This caused him to recall the death of his father. How angry he had been at his mother for having given away his father's hats.

That was thirty-two years ago, Eddie figured. New York, and again he thought about the *Caliban*. Eddie was there a lot. He stood at the closet and tried to drum up the waitress's name. It had taken him weeks to get her to say yes.

Eddie took a step into the closet and ran a finger over the fedora's brim, the black felt still soft. "Think her name began with a D," he muttered.

Eddie and D did not last long. She was too fast for him, dragging him to dance clubs where she liked to get loaded. The loaded part did not bother him as much as the loud music and sweaty crowds.

"What was that word D used to use?" Eddie asked the fedora. "Boogie, that was it: 'I wanna go out and boogie.'"

He leaned against the closet's doorjamb. Dance, he thought. Maria Cruz, remembering her name right away. He had met her not long after D. Maria had come to New York from Puerto Rico, worked in a record store and studied ballet. A single mother, she had a four-year-old daughter. They lived up in Spanish Harlem with Maria's parents.

She stayed at Eddie's a few nights a week. Sometimes she would bring her music with her and practice her ballet, wearing the fedora. While she danced Eddie would imagine the sea, its waves rolling under the moonlight.

Eddie stepped back from the closet and asked himself what had caused their breakup.

"Oh, yeah," he sighed. While going with Maria she was seeing a wealthy Park Avenue bachelor. Maria had told Eddie about him right off, and Eddie had to accept it. He did not like the alternatives: let her go or totally commit himself to her. Playing it on middle ground was best for him at the time.

He was surprised one day when his Park Avenue competition had called. He said he wanted to marry Maria. Wanted to give Maria and her whole family a better life. He pleaded for Eddie to let her go.

Eddie again leaned against the jamb. "I did it for you, Maria. For you and your little girl."

He straightened up and stared at the fedora's black brim, then lowered his eyes to the hat below, the one at the bottom of the stack. It was a cowboy hat, given to him out here in Los Angeles.

Connie was an aspiring actor from San Diego. A few days after they had met, she invited Eddie to a party at a film star's home. The hat had been worn in his last movie, which turned out to be a huge flop. He did not want to be reminded of it. That was why he had offered Eddie the hat.

It was chocolate brown, and the leather was hard. It was impossible to disturb the shape of the crown, the curl of the brim. It was good support for the hats above it.

"Connie..." Eddie said to it.

After five years together she still had not gotten anywhere with her career. Discouragement had cracked her spirit, and a bit of her mind as well.

At the oddest times while at home with her, Connie would dance naked while singing "The Good Ship Lollipop." She would wear the cowboy hat when she did this, and not once did Eddie imagine the sea with its waves rolling under the moonlight.

There had been other women in Eddie's life, vague images flipping now through his mind, fragments of lost loves.

Four hats, he thought. The Mexican one was not on the stack. The one he wanted to wear tonight. "Gretchen...

Ensenada...Dusseldorf," he mumbled as he searched behind the hanging coats and jackets. Where had it gone?

Bedroom closet, he guessed. About to leave the hall closet it came back to him. Eddie leaned a hand on the knob of the door, stood at an angle and stared thoughtfully at the floor.

Ten, twelve years ago the wind had blown it off his head. Woman's damn dog caught it and chewed a piece out of the straw brim. After that he had kept it in the trunk of his car, wore it against the sun while he worked construction jobs. Threw it away when he had become a bartender.

Eddie took his hand from the doorknob and stepped into the closet. With both hands he grasped the Panama's brim on either side, lifting it along with the Alpine that sat on top. He set the two of them aside on the shelf and pulled the black fedora off the cowboy hat.

Returning to the sofa with it, he sat and set it on his lap. Eddie could not believe he had thrown away the old Mexican hat. Should not have done that, he told himself, brim ruined or not.

The other thing he could not believe was that the movie was almost over. How could he have been with his hats so long? There was no chance Emily would call this late.

"Just as well," he said to the phone, thinking Emily would have become like all the rest—gone.

Eddie wondered then if his relationships had ended because of bad luck. No, he decided, not bad luck. It was because he had become infatuated with another, driven by passion to move on to a new heartthrob. It was now that he realized he had spent his entire life believing he deserved to have anything he wanted.

An explosion blew away his thoughts. A building had just blown up in the last scene of the movie.

A commercial came on. The young blonde in it reminded him of Carol—back in New York. How could he have forgotten about her? She had thought him so handsome in the black fedora. Carol. Bright in mind and personality.

Her parents had had a vacation home in the wooded hills of

Woodstock. Occasionally, when her parents were not there, she and Eddie would drive up and spend a few days doing nothing but loving each other.

Eddie smiled warmly at the memory of them on the upstairs veranda of the house. Where they had sat before the most glorious sunsets he had ever seen.

The glorious sunsets were no more after he left Carol. Eddie had become infatuated with yet another, one whose name he could not recall.

He raised the fedora from his lap and put it on. He pushed his thumb between the brim and the top of his right ear, and the hat tilted to its proper angle. If Eddie had been in a rakish mood, he would have used the width of two fingers to angle it even more. This was something else his father had taught him about hats.

Eddie curled the brim down over his left eye, picked up the remote and shut off the TV. His reflection reappeared on the dark screen. "You're kidding me," Eddie said to his other self. "Eddie and Emily—she finally called and they went out to what? To boogie—boogie—boogie!" and the two Eddies laughed hard together.

Eddie got off the sofa and gave his other self a wave goodbye. He went into the bathroom where he stood in front of the mirror. The black fedora gave him a dangerous look. He liked that.

At the far end of the countertop sat a small wooden bowl of shaving soap. On its lid, the soap brush rested upright on the flat base of its glass handle. Alongside the bowl, his decades-old double-edge Gillette razor, much heavier than what they make nowadays, he thought. Aside from the memories of his father, the Gillette and glass-handled brush were all he had left of him.

Eddie leaned over the tub, closed the drain stopper and turned the diverter from shower to bath. He ran the water and went into the bedroom.

Eddie returned naked, except for the black fedora on his head. He turned the water off and got into the tub. He pushed the hat forward and leaned back against the porcelain. Reaching out to the countertop he took hold of the Gillette and removed the blade.

It did not take long for the water to change color. It reminded Eddie of those glorious Woodstock sunsets. He then thought about the Mexican hat, along with all the rest he had thrown away in his time.

About the author:

Phillip Frey's history includes professional actor, produced screenwriter and writer/director of three short films, one of which showed at the New York Film Festival. He is now devoted only to writing prose. The books *Dangerous Times* and *Hym and Hur* were his first published works of fiction. He currently has the privilege of having short stories appearing in various literary journals and anthologies. amazon.com/author/phillipfrey.

THIRD PLACE

WHEN THE MOON GETS IN THE
WAY OF THE SUN
©2020 by William E. Burleson

The little rocky satellite of a satellite moved between its big brother and the local star. The star didn't care. Thus is the life of these mighty nuclear furnaces: such routine and inconsequential events don't measure a blip on their larger cosmic concerns. The local star cared even less about the random bits of stuff on the small rock about to be shadowed, including the animate beings scampering about on its surface. On the other hand, in 2017 millions of these animate beings cared enough about the coming shadow to congregate along its seventy-mile-wide path, cutting across the western hemisphere from just south of Portland to Charleston, in hopes of seeing the eclipse in its full glory.

As a result, traffic coming into St. Joseph, Missouri, sucked. Willy Boil pulled his Ford Ranger off 169 onto the exit ramp to downtown, knuckles white, teeth clenched. To Willy, it looked like everybody in America with a tank of gas was descending on the old town. He himself had driven down from Sioux Falls, South Dakota, starting out at five a.m. to beat the rush, apparently just like everyone else.

Cars lined up at the light with their right blinkers on, but Willy didn't have anywhere special to go, so he cruised up the empty left lane toward downtown. Who knows where these people are going? Willy thought. It's not like the eclipse was happening at one particular spot in tiny St. Joseph, anyplace would do just fine.

A car pulled out of line directly into his path, and Willy slammed on the brakes. He honked the angriest honk an old Ford Ranger can muster, making his tennis elbow hurt and his teeth grind even more. "Asshole!" Willy yelled, glad his windows were rolled up. The Kia Sorento continued on into downtown as if nothing happened.

Willy followed. Not to follow, but because that was where he was going. Still, Willy took the opportunity to tail a little closer than normal to show his displeasure with the ball-sack's lack of driving skill.

In the Kia Sorento, José Colon looked in his rearview mirror. Now the aggressive A-hole was following him. Sure, why not. He hadn't seen the car zooming up on the left, speeding for sure. Now the guy—were those South Dakota plates?—just had to make a big deal out of it. José continued on his route, wondering what to do if South Dakota kept it up, stopped where he stopped, maybe even wanting to fight—damn!—did the guy want to fight? José was in his late forties, and he liked to think of himself as somewhat in shape, but he also knew that was a generous assessment. His wife, who had to work and couldn't come up from the Kansas side of Kansas City, nagged him about his spare tire, one earned by a career of sitting on his ass in an office, moving EIOR forms from one basket to another. He couldn't imagine throwing punches with some hoodlum. Still, he had to be a man and he was determined to stand up to the bully. To a point.

Willy, in a moment of cosmic synchronicity, just two hours until a real moment of cosmic synchronicity, was having the same thoughts as José. The last time Willy had been in a fight was in junior high, and he got his ass kicked. Still, he was emboldened by the Kia's—were those Kansas plates?—lack of reaction. They both pulled up to a stop sign. Happily, the driver didn't get out. Willy didn't need the aggravation, so he gave Kansas a little more room on the next block. His blood pressure slowly returned to normal, or at least normal for him. The world is full of assholes, but there's no reason to let Kansas get to him. That's the kind of thing that made his wife leave, after all. She thought he was an angry man. He didn't think that fair, since it's not like he had hit her. But still, as his therapist had said, he needed to learn to use his anger constructively. He never knew what that meant.

José regretted coming. He really wanted to see the eclipse, and his wife provided her usual passive-aggressive permission, saying "Just go," but so far it had been nothing but traffic and headaches and the forecast looked pretty hopeless. But there he was; no turning back now.

At the next corner, José took a right and felt relieved to see South Dakota keep going forward.

As the Kia turned right, Willy felt relieved as well. He continued on. His GPS said there was a coffee shop up ahead, and he needed a caffeine fix and a bathroom after his long drive. He was surprised to see only a few people on the street. He didn't know what he expected, but crowds would have been a reasonable bet. All the better for him, he figured, since that meant more good places for him to see the eclipse. He looked at the sky. That is IF they can see the eclipse. It was pretty cloudy and looking cloudier every minute. Damn. Try to think positive, Willy thought, like the therapist said.

None of which was in any way relevant to the sun. The sun had bigger worries, performing a balancing act of energy and gravity for longer than any of its satellites existed. It knew that one day, billions of years in the future, that balance will change and it will consume its rockier children and, finally, die. But the sun also knew that even that event will have little cosmic significance, given it was one more star on the edge of one more galaxy in one more cluster of galaxies making up a universe too vast for one star—not to mention small planet, one beautiful shadow, or one cluster of animate beings hankering for coffee—to really matter.

In the coffee shop was a line to beat all lines. Willy sighed. First, he used the bathroom, which—miracles of miracles—was available.

Relieved, he found his place in line, or at least a place, since calling it a "line" was generous; it was more of a mob. Maybe it'll move fast, he thought. He looked at his phone, pulling up the forecast. It had deteriorated since he last checked, rain now moved up to 1:00, right when the eclipse was supposed to happen. He had to take a sick day from his miserable hardware store job to attend the once in a lifetime event, and it would be a real rip-off if he drove for seven hours to see nothing. Maybe he'd get fired, too, since who was going to believe him that he was sick. Think positive, he reminded himself. If they fired him, they'd be doing him a favor. At forty-six, working at a McJob like that was the worst.

Willy's reverie was interrupted with a bump from behind, causing him to almost drop his phone.

"Sorry, man," the twenty-something with a millennial beard said.

Willy didn't reply, instead thinking, "People suck."

Rory Kaczynski, the millennial with a beard, was, in fact, sorry, even though it wasn't his fault. A giggling teenage girl, walking and texting in the crowded café, had bumped into him, causing Rory to bump into the middle-aged guy next to him. She didn't say anything. Seemed about right, in that steamy, miserable coffee shop, mostly filled with old people in khaki's fondling their eclipse glasses. Meanwhile, the one and only barista—a fellow millennial with a man bun and tattoos up each arm, moved like an arthritic sloth despite the mayhem in front of him. Rory figured the dude picked the wrong day to torch up the ol' bong before coming to work. Rory had driven down from Minneapolis on a whim. He texted his supervisor at Quality Bicycle Parts on Sunday that he wanted to go see the eclipse, and his supervisor texted back to go for it. Now here he was, his Prius parked a block away as he suffered in line, jonesing for an Americano.

Eventually, the stoned barista made it through the plump tourist's triple mochas with sprinkles orders, and Rory was up. "I'll take a..."

"Hey, I was next." It was the middle-aged guy who he bumped

into twenty minutes earlier.

Rory was sure he was there before this guy. Wasn't he?

Willy had had enough. After waiting forever for the coffee monkey behind the counter to make it through the line, now it was his turn. Instead, the tattooed man skipped him to wait on a fellow hippie skateboard guy. Willy had noticed many times how he was increasingly invisible, whether it's getting cut off earlier or being bumped into in line as if he wasn't even there. Now that same hippie cutting in front of him in line? No, no way. He was next. He was pretty sure, anyway.

"Oh, Are you sure?" Rory said.

"Yeah, I'm sure," Willy replied with a bark.

"Fine, but you don't have to be a douche about it." Why do people have to be like that?

"You butt in ahead of me, and I'm the douche," Willy said under his breath, but intending to be heard.

The stoned barista stood blinking, unsure what to do.

"I didn't butt in. I think you're the one butting in. But hey! That's ok. You are an important man. Please, be my guest!" Rory said in the best sarcastic tone he could muster. Rory felt proud of finding a creative way to make fun of the old fart-sack.

Willy didn't like being made fun of, but he did like winning. The barista got him his coffee and Willy paid without anything more said. Outside, fumbling with his key before getting in his Ranger, Willy asked himself, Why, why, why are there so many assholes in the world?

The sun's nuclear furnace created weather that no simple flesh and blood beings could possibly survive or even truly fathom. The sun churned and boiled, offering cold spots followed by great leaping flairs into the cosmos. It didn't care—that's how the sun rolls: violent, extreme, cataclysmic, but yet enjoying billions of years of yellow equilibrium. It certainly didn't care about the so-called weather on its third child, that in certain places clouds of water vapor would obstruct the animate inhabitants' enjoyment of the sun and the coming shadow.

Which is to say, that at twelve-thirty, it started to drizzle in St. Joseph. Willy was slowly resigning himself to the whole thing being a bust. Still, there was nothing to do but see it through. It's not over until it's over, and all that. He drove down the main street looking for a good spot. He came across a parking ramp. It looked empty. Perfect! He pulled in and wove his way up the three stories to the top deck, and when he got to the top, he could see the top of the ramp wasn't empty, it was half full of people who had the same idea. Some seed-cap guys stood behind an SUV, drinking beers in the rain, not looking up. A South-Asian family of four looked up at the sky, disappointment evident on the faces of the little kids. A couple of college student types tossed a Frisbee around with a complete lack of skill. Most people were staying in their cars to keep out of the rain. Still, there was plenty of room, and Willy parked. He got out, walked to the front of his truck, and peered up at the rain clouds. Even though the sun was completely obscured, he put on his eclipse glasses he had ordered from Amazon, just to do it. He couldn't see a thing. Shit.

In the very next car, José sat, depressed, wipers on. He had picked his glasses up at the office; they were giving them away for free. Now they sat on the dashboard. He saw a small truck pull in on his left. He couldn't believe it! That South Dakota asshole parked right next to him! José watched the guy get out. The guy must be looking for trouble! But he didn't make any threatening moves, instead, the middle-aged guy walked to the front of his truck, looked up at the sky, and put on his eclipse glasses. What a moron, José thought, there's no sun. José didn't know what to do. Could it just be a coincidence he pulled in right next to him? Maybe. Seemed like it. How long until South Dakota recognizes him from before? His fight or flight kicked in, more flight than fight. Screw it, he thought, why not go somewhere else? Who needs the hassle? Hell, just go home, nothing to see here anyway.

He put his car into reverse, backing into a Prius rolling by.

"Shit!" yelled Rory in the Prius.

"*Joder!*" screamed José.

"Whoa!" Willy said upon hearing that distinctive sound of fenders bending. He took off his eclipse glasses. Hey, he thought, is that the Kansas Kia from earlier?

José got out and walked around his car in the rain, surveying it from stem to stern. He didn't want to look up at the driver, being rattled and unsure of what would happen next. He found his plastic back bumper puckered in. "Oh, shit!" He felt a little better when he saw that the Prius got the worst of it, with a long crack up the front bumper cover.

Rory got out. "What the hell, man? You just pull out without looking?"

José looked up. "What? You in a hurry? You're driving in a parking ramp, you dope!"

Rory walked to the front of his car, stood next to José, and looked at the crack in the fiberglass or whatever plastic they make Prius bumpers out of. He pointed at it. "Ah, shit, man!"

"Look at mine!" José yelled and pointed himself.

"It's your fault!"

"What? What are you talking about? You ran into me!"

Willy walked over, knowing he was officially a witness to an accident even though he didn't see a thing. Plus, he wanted to see if the Kia had South Dakota plates. Up close to the two yelling and gesturing men, he saw that the Prius guy was that dildo from the coffee shop.

Rory saw Willy walking up, and, not recognizing him from earlier, thought this was a good guy to recruit to his side. "Look what that dipshit did to my car!"

"Look what this jackass did to *my* car!" José said, hoping that South Dakota still didn't remember him.

Willy stood next to them, feeling happy. They deserve each other, he thought. He scratched his chin. "Doesn't look too bad," he said. "At least they're drivable."

Willy looked over the Kia and saw the Kansas plates. "Hey, aren't you the dickweed who almost ran into me?"

"I didn't almost hit you; you were driving like a maniac!"

Rory looked Willy over. "Hey, aren't you the crank from the coffee shop?" He threw his hands up in the air in a universal sign of resignation. "Just great: the dude who can't wait his turn is the only witness to this creep busting up my car."

"You're the one who can't wait his turn!" Willy said. "And I didn't see the accident, anyway."

"Oh, sure, you were standing right there, and you didn't see this putz bash my car in. I get it."

"I had on my..." Willy started to say, waving his cardboard glasses around.

"Hey, this was all your fault! Don't try to worm your way out of it!" José said, pointing at his bumper.

And so, they argued, in no particular order, about codes of conduct on the road and in coffee shops, about bumpers and bashing into each other in parking ramps. And as they did, they didn't notice two things. First, the crowd of gawkers gathering, mouths agape, some carrying beers and some with children in tow, and one with a Frisbee, forming a circle around the increasingly aggressive men. The second thing they didn't notice was the rain slow and finally stop.

One thing led to another and the pushing began. No one could recall later who started it. One guy pushed another guy who pushed another guy and on and on. With no clear order or alliances, the three possessing neither an exit strategy nor ability to win a three-way fight, the tussle resembled less mortal combat and more an awkward display of square dancing punctuated with vulgarities and threats of bodily harm.

The light disappeared, more like a dimmer switch than a sunset. Willy was the first to notice and look up. Rory pushed José and looked up as well. José saw what the other men were doing and looked to the sky himself. Then, in a stroke of good luck or divine intervention—depending who you'd ask later—the clouds parted.

At that moment, the moon speeding along its well-defined

course, got between St. Joseph and the uncaring star, and the seventy-mile-wide shadow fell over the three men and the circle of spectators.

A cheer erupted from down in the street. Somewhere someone set off fireworks. The people on the top floor of the parking ramp—beer drinkers, Frisbee players, and fighters alike—all just looked up.

Not only was the mighty sun far above the parking ramp in St. Joseph, Missouri, North America, Earth unconcerned about the tiny moon blocking its brilliance, it cared even less about the boring squabbles of three cranky men. It had bigger issues on its cosmic mind. However, to the animate inhabitants of that particular piece of rock standing on the top of a parking ramp, the shadow mattered. They stood in awe, looking up at the great eclipsed star, the corona forming a ring seemingly just out of reach, yet beyond comprehension. The beauty, the power, the perspective was not lost on the parking lot dwellers nor anyone else in the shadow. Together, they stood in lockstep solidarity with their newly won awareness of their inconsequence.

Finally, the first rays of the minor star peeked out from behind the minor moon of the minor planet onto the town of St. Joseph. The people on the parking ramp put on their eclipse glasses and watched as the sun slowly reappeared. After they finally grew bored and stiff-necked, the three men took off their glasses and looked at each other. No one spoke. Rory looked at his bumper. Willy folded up his eclipse glasses and put them in his shirt pocket. Jose shrugged. And the three men got in their vehicles and drove back to their different worlds without more being said.

About the author:

William E Burleson's short stories have appeared in numerous literary journals and anthologies to date, including *The New Guard* and *American Fiction 14* and *16*. He is now working on a novel, *Ahnwee Days*, the story of a small town that has seen better days and the mayor who tries to save it. Burleson also has published extensively in non-fiction, most notably his book, *Bi America* (Haworth Press, 2005), as well as for the *Hennepin History Magazine* and numerous other publications. Burleson is also the founder of Flexible Press; whose recent work includes the novel *Under Ground* and the anthologies *Home* and *Lake Street Days*. For examples of past work and more information, visit www.williamburleson.com.

AN ABEYANCE
©2020 by Theresa Jenner Garrido

The torn Pepsi-Cola sign tacked to the screen door of Willa's Café flapped in the cold December wind. The bite in the morning air promised an early winter. Peter Gregg held the café door open, and his pretty companion quickly stepped in.

Although late for breakfast and early for lunch, a dozen or so men sat at the counter, drinking steaming cups of Willa McDaniel's strong coffee. Chattering families filled the booths that lined the windows, enjoying Sunday-after-church brunches. Behind the register, a radio played a snappy melody as Peter, spying an empty booth in the corner by the restroom, gently pushed the girl ahead of him.

"Not my first choice, but it'll have to do. Sorry, Sarah," he murmured.

"Oh, it's all right. We're lucky to have found a table at all."

"Yeah. Willa's is a popular place, for sure."

Peter scooted in on one side, and she slid in across from him, first taking care to brush away crumbs from the seat. Sarah grimaced at a long tear in the vinyl, haphazardly mended with strips of black tape—a catch-all for stray morsels, ashes and dirt.

Peter noticed her distaste. "Is it really okay, honey?"

Sarah looked up at his concerned expression and rolled her eyes. "Yes, of course. I'm not Princess Elizabeth." When he grinned, she made a face. "Stop laughing at me." Her right hand made a futile attempt to straighten her tousled, wind-blown curls. "I must look like a scarecrow." Her voice betrayed a touch of embarrassment as she rummaged in her pocketbook for comb and mirror.

"Prettiest scarecrow I ever saw," Peter returned with a chuckle.

She wrinkled her nose and tossed the purse aside. "Oh, well, I shouldn't be primping at the table anyway, and certainly shouldn't be so vain. I am what I am."

"Honey, nothing in this world can outshine you...except maybe a cheese omelet. I'm starved."

She would have stuck her tongue out at him if the waitress hadn't chosen that moment to hurry over with glasses of water, silverware and menus.

"There, darlings. I'll be back in a jiff," the buxom girl drawled, handing them each a dog-eared menu.

Peter immediately opened his and studied it with anticipation. Sarah perused hers half-heartedly. The smell of strong coffee, permeating the entire room, along with the odor of frying grease, was doing a number on her stomach. She'd never been fond of breakfasts out, but Peter wanted a bite after church before they headed out to the farm to visit his grandparents.

It seemed churlish to object to such a small thing, especially when they were to be married in less than a month. Everything was going so well, too; no mishaps with reservations or caterers or bridesmaids. She could afford to be generous and amenable.

Eyebrows in a knot, she scanned the menu a second time. Eggs, sausage and toast...waffle and syrup...pancakes and blueberry sauce.... Nothing appealed to her or sounded remotely appetizing. With a sigh, she closed the menu and folded her hands.

"Decide on anything, Sarah?"

"Oh, Peter...I'm really not very hungry. I think I'll just have some hot cocoa."

"You have to eat more than that. How about pancakes?"

"Ohh, after the syrup soaks in, they're nothing but doughy globs. I don't like pancakes, Peter. You know that."

"Well, then, how about an egg with a side of bacon and some raisin bread toast with jam or honey?"

She shook her head. "No, Peter, I just can't. Please. I'll have a doughnut with the cocoa, but nothing else. And you know your grandmother probably has a huge, delicious dinner planned, so I'll need plenty of room for that."

Peter grinned. "Okay. You're right. But even so, I'm going to have an omelet and a side of ham. Maybe some hash browns."

She rolled her eyes. "Go ahead. Don't know where you put it, though. If I ate as much as you, I'd be bigger than Melva Creek over at the Mercantile."

The waitress returned with pencil and tablet, and Peter gave their order. After she sashayed away, he reached across the table and took Sarah's hand in a firm grasp. She smiled and basked for a moment in the warm glow of their mutual happiness.

"Oh, Peter...isn't it wonderful your grandparents have decided to give you the farm?"

"Oh, yeah."

"We didn't expect such good fortune. Later, yes...after we'd been married a while...but not now."

"Gramps said he likes being overseer of his own will. Said it was better to bequeath it now than after he was dead and buried. He was busting with pleasure over surprising me."

"Well, his generous surprise is certainly giving *us* pleasure. Just think. Starting out our married life in that beautiful old house. It has seen so many years of happiness."

"Yep. My dad and uncles sure enjoyed growing up there, though they had their ups and downs."

"Of course, they did, but what are a few ups and downs? Everyone goes through bad times now and then. I mean, we weathered a few ourselves." She tossed her head. "But that's all behind us. Let's you and me only think of the good years ahead of us. We're young and healthy, and you have a good steady job, and now the farm and—goodness! I think we're about the luckiest people on the earth."

"That we are, Sarah, my girl."

Sarah leaned forward, her eyes dancing. "And guess what? Your grandmother is going to divulge her close-kept secret and show me how to make that luscious apple butter and how to put-up peaches and plums."

"That's great, Sarah. Don't know what her secret is, but her apple butter is the best in five states. Always wins a blue at the county fair." He grinned. "Oh, forgot to tell you. John is coming over next weekend, and he and Gramps are going to help me paint the house and patch the shed roof. Grams and Gramps want to be out and in the cottage by the first of January...before any big storms hit."

"That will give us two weeks to move in. Plenty of time, don't you think?"

"Heavens yes. John's asked two of his buddies to help with the heavy stuff, so we'll be settled in no time. Since my grandparents are leaving us a lot of their furniture, we haven't much to move in."

"Your brother John is such a great guy."

"Yep, he sure is."

"And I'm thrilled to have some of those wonderful pieces of maple furniture. The huge dining room table...the sideboard...and those braided rugs. My gosh. They're worth a pretty penny."

"Grams and Aunt Martha made those rugs, you know."

"I know, and they are awesome works of art." Sarah lifted her shoulders and uttered a tiny squeal. "Ohh, Peter," she sighed. "I'm getting more excited by the minute. At this rate, I may burst."

"Swell. Maybe we should just elope and—"

Peter's sentence was cut short and his attention diverted when the waitress appeared with their plates. After a brief prayer of thanks, he dove in with good appetite, but Sarah couldn't bring herself to even take a nibble of the plump, sugar-dusted doughnut. Instead, she watched her fiancé as he eagerly devoured bite after bite of fluffy omelet. A good thing she knew how to cook because the way to her beloved's heart was definitely through his stomach. She giggled.

"Peter...do you know what Eileen Simms asked me the other day?"

Peter's fork paused in mid-air. "No, what did that silly goose ask you?"

"She asked if we planned to take your old runabout on our

honeymoon. And I told her we planned to drive it all the way to Niagara Falls."

"Niagara Falls?"

"Yes. That's where most people go on their honeymoon, you know."

"In *our* runabout?"

"That's what was so funny. You should've seen her face. She just stared at me as if I were crazy."

"Poor Eileen. You shouldn't be such a tease. You know how gullible she is. Besides, we're not going to Niagara Falls."

"Oh, pooh. I know we're not, but she shouldn't ask so many questions. As if I would tell her, of all people, where we were going on our honeymoon, in the first place."

"And in my runabout, no less."

She giggled. "Yes, in your runabout."

Peter grinned and focused on his meal. Willa had turned up the volume on the radio and music flooded the small café.

"Does she always have the radio going like that?" Sarah asked between sips of her cooling cocoa.

"Honey, Willa hasn't missed a radio program in umpteen years. Keeps that infernal box on all day. Nobody seems to mind. Everybody likes the music. Helps digestion."

"That's not what your grandmother would say. Why, she'd die before she'd allow the radio on during a meal."

"She's old-fashioned. But don't let her holier-than-thou air fool you. When nobody is looking, that woman is soaking up every soap opera on the air. I overheard her listening to one a few years back, but she doesn't know I know. Would ruin her saintly image."

"You're kidding. Not your strict grandmother. A soap opera? How funny."

Peter chuckled, and Sarah shook with half-smothered giggles. The man in the next booth turned to stare, so she quickly bit into her doughnut for relief. The thought of Peter's grandmother, captivated by a heart-rending, tear-jerking serial, was too much, and she wondered how she'd manage a straight face that afternoon at the farm. One look at the older lady, and Sarah would surely burst into laughter.

"You better behave yourself, Sarah-my-love, or Grams will think you've gone off your rocker."

"Oh, it's silly, isn't it? But it struck me so funny." She took a swallow of water and let out a sigh. "I'll catch hold of myself. I promise. I'll act every bit my age and be every inch a lady...as befitting an engaged woman, about to be married."

"Eat your doughnut."

"I am. You finish your ham."

"I'm trying to. But it's hard to chew when your girl is drowning in giggles."

"I've stopped."

"After we're married, it might be wise if we didn't eat breakfast out together."

"Peter Gregg!"

"Eat your doughnut."

"I'm so happy, I can't think of food right now."

"Sarah-girl, you amaze me."

"Do I really?"

Peter shook his head and drained his cup of coffee. Sarah smiled and sat back with an air of complete satisfaction. She listened as the radio played a beautiful orchestral arrangement of a familiar classic. She looked at the many contented faces sitting around her. They appeared happy but were any as completely happy as she?

Willa, leaning on the counter, chatted with a young man in uniform as he sipped a cup of coffee. She chewed her gum in time with the music, and Sarah felt more giggles stir. That was another thing Grams wouldn't allow. Gum chewing. Uncouth and the product of the devil, she said. Sarah swallowed her mirth. The dear old gal probably chewed gum on the sly, too.

"Peter, isn't life simply full of wonderful things?"

"Yes, I suppose it is."

"Remind me to tell your grandmother what a dear I think she

is."

"She already knows you like her. She thinks you're a dear, too, Sarah." He winked. "And, so do I."

"Oh, Peter, I think we—"

Before Sarah could finish her sentence, a strident voice on the radio shocked the small café into silence.

We interrupt this program to bring you a special news bulletin. The Japanese have attacked Pearl Harbor, Hawaii by air, President Roosevelt has just announced. The attack was also made on all naval and military activities on the principal island of Oahu...

About the author:

Born and raised in the beautiful Pacific Northwest, Theresa attended the University of Washington, received a B.A. in English, and spent the next twenty-plus years teaching middle school language arts, drama, and social studies before retiring "early." The author of over thirty novels, Theresa enjoys painting, reading and traveling with her retried engineer husband. She currently resides in South Carolina

HOLY SPIRIT DELIVERS
©2020 by Nancy Canyon

Roger and I are sitting on the front porch enjoying the evening sky pinking up. It's almost time to go to meeting and tonight I hope to succeed in expressing the Lord. Despite Roger's reassurance that I'll do fine, goosebumps tickle my forearms when I think about standing up front of the congregation. I'm afraid something bad will happen. Perhaps the Devil will inhabit me instead of the Lord. Roger calls this kind of thinking, *Jimjam*. He doesn't buy it for a second that there is evil in the world. I want to say, *Just look around you*, but I don't.

Dust rises above the grove near the highway. "Not expecting anyone, are you?"

Roger picks at his guitar, but says nothing.

I shrug. "Everyone's saying it's my time to be filled with the glory of God, but I'm not sure about it."

"You're a hard nut to crack," Roger says, flipping his hair off his face.

That hair (and his eyes) get to me still. Shiny and black and a little unkempt. I feel a tightening deep inside when he smiles at me. I can't help it.

The moon's rising; almost full and a weird shade of pink, like a Hostess Sno Ball. And there's a crispness in the air that wasn't there last week. My fall jumper is perfect for the turning season. "How do I look?"

"Downhome," Roger says.

"That's exactly what I'm going for," I say. "I can have a visitation from HS whenever I want, you know. I'm just not sure if I'm ready yet."

"It's up to you." Roger strums *Stairway to Heaven* with his pick-like fingernails.

His thin lips concentrate into a line. I love to kiss that line, but tonight I won't be kissing anyone, 'cept the Lord, that is. He watches me smooth the jumper over my ample hips. I'm about to smile when I hear the sound of a car engine whirring up the road. "Who's coming?"

"Who do you think?"

Pastor Joe climbs from his car. He's here to make sure I'm going to church. I know this by the serious look on his face. Roger speaks in tongues regularly. Doesn't have to do nothing but close his eyes and say a prayer and he's there. Whenever I give it a go, I say something stupid like *cooked carrots, steamed squash, boiled peas, mashed potatoes.* Last time I attempted; Roger smirked. "Hey," I said, "that's all I got."

Pastor's wearing black as usual. Dust streaks his jeans from backwoods house calls. "Roger," he says, nodding. "Naomi."

I smile and cross my arms over my chest. I'm thinking an offering would be nice; perhaps the pastor could have brought me a plate of Jesus Grahams or Christ Cookies with the red jelly beans representing His blood.

"Roger, I've come to take Naomi to church this evening. I'll help her fill up right-like with Holy Spirit. Maybe she won't feel so intimidated if you're not vocalizing over the holy oil vessel all evening. Perhaps you could skip tonight's meeting."

Frowning, Roger sets down his guitar. He opens his mouth to speak, but I interrupt.

"I'm right here, in case you didn't notice," I say. "Why don't you ask me if I want to go?"

"Sorry, Naomi."

"Not tonight," I say, and turn and walk back inside the house.

I go to my stash and unwrap a Twinkie. I gobble it down, deciding to give my own little revival meeting a stab. I brush crumbs from my mouth and clear my throat. "Behold the glory of the Holy Spirit," I say, attempting tongues. I throw back my head and spout, *"Roast beef, broccoli, peaches, wheat berries."* Crumpling to the floor, I cry, "What the, what the...." rolling back and forth, ending up on my side, sighing. "Okay HS, I give up."

Roger walks in, lighting his hash pipe as he shuffles toward me. He holds his breath, eyes ablaze with glory.

I glare at him. "I'll work my ass off to get a visitation," I say. "But not for Pastor. Something weird about that dude. You believe in me, don't you?"

Releasing the smoke in a giant cloud, he says, "Sure I do, Naomi. Sure I do."

Roger remains on the porch long after dusk, strumming his guitar beneath the bright moon. It's his habit to sit around a campfire and watch the stars come out. Says it makes him feel connected to a greater whole. Like when he lived by the river. That's when we first met. I was walking the neighbor's dog and stumbled across a clutch of hobos eating beans and Little Smokies. They offered me a plate and I took them up on it.

Roger said I looked wholesome. I said he looked honorable. We met up every evening after that, sitting around the fire, watching the stars, smelling of smoke and the river by dawn. Then he invited me to church. Said he spoke in tongues and that Holy Spirit strengthened him. He wanted me to give it a try. I told him I had my own way of communing with Spirit.

After Roger moved into the farmhouse I inherited from Gramps, I learned that he was regularly filled and animated by Holy Spirit. Unlike me, he doesn't need church-window cookies, lace cookies, spirit knots, and Lord's kisses to feel connected. But since Jesus Christ is a cookie eater himself, I know I'm properly aligned. I heard that once He gave someone a plateful of sugar cookies. They could tell the cookies were from Him because He'd taped a picture of Himself atop the Saran Wrap cover.

I'm sure I'm being filled with His glory in my own personal way. But you should never do anything counter to your sweetheart, right? Wrong.

Sarah Lee. Mrs. Smith. Betty Crocker. There's nothing in the Good Book saying *Thou shalt not eat banana cream pie.* Nor is there anything saying *Thou shalt rise up embodied with spinach.*

Ha! Roger's unaware of the stash stuffed beneath my side of the bed: Twinkies, Ding Dongs, Sno Balls, Ho Hos, and Devil Dogs. When I wake in the night worrying about my lack of charisma, I grab a treat and soon the Divine enters me fully.

At the next meeting, Roger and I plant ourselves in the back row of Pastor Joe's revival tent. Reverent voices heap up and press down. By the time the basket passes, I'm imagining fudge melting on my tongue. I even stir the bills with my fingers, thinking I might find cookies zipped inside sandwich bags beneath the offering, but I only find ones and fives and tens. Pastor calls up the wounded, the sinful, and the sorry of heart. A tall man with narrow eyes and flat features zombies up the aisle. I don't recognize him from around these parts, but Roger perks up immediately. It isn't long before the man swoons, is caught and let down gently onto the carpeted aisle. I'm afraid I won't recognize Holy Spirit when he comes. I press my lips together, hoping nothing embarrassing will leave this mouth.

Roger stands. "Come on," he says, and takes my hand.

"Wait!" I hold back, but he doesn't let go, and soon we're squeezing past folks seated in the row of folding chairs. As we stumble into the center aisle, I whisper, "Maybe the pastor will smear a holy oil cross on my forehead and be done with it."

Pastor says Holy Spirit is everywhere: on street corners, at the Laundromat, even behind the counter at Ace Hardware. *Jesus Cookies*, I think, certain that my habit fills and expresses Holy Spirit through me as completely as He animates Roger's tongue. Roger continues with his prompting and shortly I'm standing at the front facing happy-to-see-me Pastor Joe.

"This is Naomi's first time speaking in tongues," he bellows to the congregation. The congregation cheers.

Fidgeting, I turn to the full house beaming love and encouragement at me. Grimacing, I turn back to Pastor Joe.

"Relax, Naomi," he says, and touches oil to my forehead.

I squeal like a river rat. The strange sound brings on a fit of laughter. Soon, I'm side-splitting out of control. Guffaws have me doubled over. I lose control, releasing Roger's hand with the force of my gales, until I'm flailing on the floor, convulsing with hilarity. Mass hysteria erupts throughout the congregation and the joy meter reaches volcanic. Then it's over, and I work to catch my breath. I roll on my side, dabbing at my eyes. My belly hurts.

The moon is full, shining brightly through the bedroom window. Tonight, there is no orange tint, just straight on Hostess Sno Ball. Roger's silent, angry at me still, I guess. Thinking I was faking it, he bolted from the sanctuary. Pastor caught up with him later, explaining that Holy Spirit inhabited me in my own special way. *What a nut case, that HS.*

Roger begins to snore and I reach over the side of the bed, feeling around for a Christ Cake—nothing. I hang over the edge of the mattress and peer beneath. Nothing but shadows and lint.

What the hell did you do with my stash? I want to shout, but Roger's snoring full-on now. Then I have this queer idea—maybe HS absorbed the goods while I was consumed with laughter, turning them into light or fire or some such magical nonsense. Settling back against my pillow, I feel a great pressure gripping my chest. In the moonlight I see a blue light hovering above my feet. It begins to take on the shape of a mound of Twinkies. As I watch the vision undulate, tears spring to my eyes. At last, I'm home.

About the author:

Artist/author, Nancy Canyon, MFA, creates in a vintage art studio/gallery in Historic Fairhaven, Bellingham, WA. Her paintings, photographs, poems, and prose are widely published: *True Stories II, Raven Chronicles, Water~Stone Review, Fourth*

Genre, Floating Bridge Review, Clover: A Literary Rag, Bellingham Review, Cirque, Nature's Healing Spirit, and more. Her novel, *Celia's Heaven,* is forthcoming from Penchant Press, 2020. Nancy works as a writing coach for The Narrative Project. Additionally, she teaches writing and the illustrated journal for Chuckanut Writers in Bellingham, WA. She has written a memoir manuscript detailing two summers spent as a fire lookout attendant in the Clearwater National Forest in the early 70s. She is married with three grown children, a cat and a dog. She loves to dance and laugh with her friends, and to spend time in nature.

PEARL
©2020 by Michelle Wotowiec

His name is Jeffrey and he wears his pants a little too high and his shirts a little too-tucked in, reminds me of an old man. He tells me, one night after we have finished and have our bodies intertwined, that he likes to close his eyes and picture moonscapes. What are moonscapes? I ask, and he tells me they're gray landscapes with endless crevices and beautiful blue skylines. I want to tell him that he is picturing clichés and there really isn't anything too unique about this image of his, it probably originates from a postcard somewhere, but I don't say that out loud. Instead I put my head on the dip below his armpit and pretend my father, who would die if he saw me now, has his own campsite on the moon—complete with a one-person tent, a fire pit, marshmallows, and some Hershey's chocolate.

Jeffrey is nothing like my father. Jeffrey sees the good in people. He even rescued a stray cat from over on Van Buren, for Christ's sake. Dad never would have done that. Dad always said that I needed to watch my back—that the world is full of bad people who want to take advantage of me. Mom, poor Mom, tried to offset Dad's negativity, but to no avail. *It isn't all bad,* she would whisper into my ears on the nights Dad fell asleep on the couch, drunk.

Jeffrey, unlike my father, doesn't know I am sixteen years old. Given, we have never actually discussed my age, but I am sure he assumes I am at least eighteen. I wear my clothes tight, showing just enough midriff to say I am way too confident to be a minor, and my make-up is on point. Jeffrey is in management over at the tile company on Smith Road. I am not sure how old he is, either, but he has mentioned that he has been with the company for over

20 years—so there's that. I would rather be wrapped in the arms of an older, successful man, than of my father's sticky alcohol-smelling skin.

We met the same day I gave my statement to the police about the accident at home. I couldn't bear to look at my mother, who was handcuffed against the far wall, so I skedaddled out of there as soon as I could and basically ran across the street to the coffee shop that was known for serving old coffee and stale pastries. Jeffrey held the door for me. I smiled. I ordered a stale croissant and a coffee black (even though I don't drink coffee), and sat at the booth in the back. Jeffrey was sitting at the table next to me before I had time to take my first crunchy bite. *Nice weather today, isn't it?* he said. His voice was deep and his salt and pepper facial hair was groomed. We chatted about the weather for a bit and I tried my hardest to make my laugh sound sincere and took pleasure in how his eyes continued to make their way down to my chest (in his defense, I was wearing my best pushup bra).

Once, early in our courtship, he asked me what I thought was the meaning of life. It took me by surprise, as up to that point everything I knew about him pointed to the mundane personality of someone who never dared to color outside the lines. His favorite restaurant was Applebee's, for Christ's sake. I didn't tell him my own theory and instead asked him what he thought was the meaning. *To enjoy every minute to the fullest,* he said. His lips curled into a smile, and he kissed me for the first time right there in the middle of Kiwanis Park, surrounded by geese and small frolicking children.

The kiss? It was great. His lips were firm and his tongue tasted like the banana bread Nana used to make on the weekends.

Jeffrey has a cellphone but doesn't really know how to use it. His text that night read, *Had a wonderful time w/ U,* followed by a winking emoji. I could tell it took him a long time to type it based on how long it said "typing" on the second text, which said, *Hope 2 C U soon beautiful.* Now, I know enough about men that it is always best to keep them wanting more, so I decided not to respond to him until the following morning. Let him think about me all night long.

Jeffrey doesn't know that I live with my older sister now. I moved in with her two days after the accident at home and, man, that girl is such a bitch. She was the planned child that my parents had in their early twenties. I was the accident that happened fifteen years later, when Mom thought she was going through menopause. *Who gets pregnant in their late thirties?* I remember her laughing with some friends over wine when I was a kid. The story goes that Dad wasn't happy about it—he was three short years from freedom (when my sister would leave for college) and wasn't thrilled about having to start the whole parenting thing all over again. That is probably why he never treated me like a daughter.

My sister, though. She thinks she knows me. Thinks she can control me—give me a fucking 9 pm curfew. She even tries to tell me what I am allowed to wear. Fucking batshit crazy that one. She works the nightshift over at Mercy Hurst, though, so I get away with what I want. When I decided I was going to have sex with Jeffrey, I wanted to do it in a familiar, safe place. Not at his place, which I hadn't even been to yet. I decided I wanted to do it on a Tuesday, so I told him he could meet me at my place at ten. He came with flowers and a bottle of champagne, so I am sure he knew what I was thinking. He said my house reminded him of his college years, but I didn't ask him to clarify. I let him take me in my sister's bed and didn't bother cleaning up the sheets.

When he was leaving that night, he kissed me, hard, and told me he wanted to see me again.

I have a few rules about men. The first is that any man can be controlled if you figure out what it is he wants and if you're comfortable enough to tease him with it. The second is that men get bored quickly, so it is important to keep things spicy. The third is that you should be prepared for hell freezing over when you're ready to leave them behind—their egos really can't handle it.

I wasn't ready to leave Jeffrey behind, yet, as it turned out he was pretty good company and he loved showering me with pretty much anything I wanted. He had a new necklace, perfume, or clothing article for me basically every time I came to his place. We had a game where I would model them for him before we went to the bedroom. That really got him going—me prancing around in nothing but the pearl necklace or ACDC tank top (bought on Amazon, not from the vendor, of course) with a spritz of Beyoncé's latest perfume line.

Back at home, my sister was turning things up a notch. She thought it'd be best if I saw a therapist to talk things through. *You can get past this,* became her catch phrase. *There's nothing to get past,* I always respond, but then she just hugs me or cries or screams.

Jeffrey is getting a bit needy. What were once text messages every few days have become text messages every couple of hours. And he gets all pissy if I don't respond right away. *Were you with someone else?* Or *Are you mad at me?* He's as bad as the boys at school. I decide to ignore him for a few days until he settles down. My sister is surprised when we are out at lunch and I don't have my phone with me. I don't tell her that I just can't bear to see another fucking text message from Jeffrey—she thinks I am making progress in my "recovery". *Disconnecting,* she says, is an important step in restarting. Whatever the fuck that means.

I finally cave and see the therapist my sister lined up. Not that I need to see one, but if it will get my sister off my back, it's worth the one hour every Thursday afternoon.

Tell me about yourself, the man who barely looks old enough to have graduated college says to me from behind a red notepad. His legs are crossed and his shirt accents his biceps. *When did you first start feeling inappropriate around your father?*

I decide I miss Jeffrey. He says we should start over. Try a new route to keep things interesting and to take our time. He invites me to play trivia with him and some of his friends at McCoy's on

Friday night. It doesn't sound like a terrible idea—again, anything to get out of the house and my sister's bullshit.

I meet him at his place beforehand. I wore my tight black dress with vanilla heals and the pearls he gave me. I can tell he wants to eat me up the moment he opens the door, but he remains a gentleman and offers me a beer. I tell him we can skip trivia and go straight to the bedroom, but he says that he wants to take me out. So, we walk over to McCoy's and get a table for five. He scoots his chair close to mine and places his hand on my thigh. *I have missed you,* he mouths with a smile and walks up to the bar to get us both a drink.

I see his friends coming in to my right. The first two men look surprisingly handsome, but older than Jeffrey. They both have near perfect jawlines and walk with confidence—I bet they would have been lady killers in their prime. They see Jeffrey at the bar and stop to talk. Jeffrey points back at me and the two men look my way. I suddenly feel very small. Misplaced. The third friend slips from behind the other two and I recognize him immediately. I feel lightheaded.

Suzie? he asks, coming to the table. He is Roland, my father's close friend from college. Before I know it, I am on my way out the door, walking as fast as I can to the bus stop three corners down.

The thing nobody knows is that I started it. I started it with my father. You see, my father was never really a father to me and the older I grew, the more of a stranger he became. It was as if the closer and closer I got to womanhood, the further he slipped away. I needed him. I loved him. He was absolutely horrified the first time I placed my hand on his inner thigh. He slammed me against the wall and called me a little whore. I cried, crumpled on the floor. It was a real cry, not the kind of cries I use for attention when I want it. I really did love him. My crying must have made him feel bad, because he came down on the floor next to me and held me in his arms.

This isn't right, he said to me on more than one occasion.

But I love you.

That isn't the right kind of love, Suzie.

Months passed before our relationship went in the direction I wanted it to and everything would have been fine—I would have had a father who loved me the way I needed him to, but one afternoon when we were in the house alone, Roland made a surprise visit and caught us on the couch. Now don't get the wrong impression about Roland. He isn't innocent. In fact, we almost hooked up a year before in the bathroom at a Browns game. He would tell the story as me luring him into the bathroom like a little harlot, which may be partially true, but he did kiss me. With tongue.

When Roland told my mother about finding us on the couch, she went ballistic. She turned into a rabid animal right in front of my eyes. I had no idea she had it in her to shoot him or I probably wouldn't have started it all in the first place.

The thing about death is that it cuts the story off in its tracks. I'm not sure how Roland saw it, but my mother was under the impression that my father was a rapist. That he took me against my will. That I am some child who was taken advantage of.

I take the bus back home and find my sister curled up on the couch with a hot chocolate and a Dean Koontz book. I want to tell her that she reads crap, but I decide not to waste my breath.

You're home early, she says.

The study group was very productive, I lie.

Come, sit. She pats the couch cushion to her left, taking note of my tight black dress and heels.

I'll stand, I say, staying in the kitchen.

Are you ready to talk about things yet, Suzie? It has been almost two months since the accident and she is growing impatient with me.

There's nothing to talk about.

How are things going with the therapist?

They're going, I lie. I know exactly what the therapist wants to hear and the whole thing is a complete waste of time.

Well, you know I am here for you, right?

She means it, I know. But she has never been much of a sister. Being so much older, she long forgot what it was like to be my age. She never took the time to acknowledge how much more our parents loved her than me. That she was the planned, perfect baby and I was the mistake, pain-in-the-ass baby that took away their retirement years.

I'm going upstairs, I say. I go to my bedroom and lock the door. I check my phone and see eight missed texts from Jeffrey. *Where did you go? Are you okay? Are you mad at me? Can I see you?* And so forth.

I'm only half surprised when I hear the doorbell ring. I make my way down the steps and watch as my sister opens the door and sees Jeffrey.

Yes? She says.

I am here to see Suzie.

Excuse me?

I am here to see Suzie.

And you are?

Jeffrey.

Are you her teacher?

*Teacher? No. I'm her—*And at that moment, Jeffrey finally puts two and two together.

You need to leave. You do know she is only sixteen, don't you?

I don't need to hear anymore. I go back to my bedroom and lock the door.

A month passes. Then another. And another. I continue to go to therapy and I even start to be a little more honest about the kind of person I am attracted to. The therapist says it all makes sense based on my history and that my attraction meter is going to be whack for a long time. I just need to stay in touch with what is real, what makes sense, and what doesn't.

One morning I wake to a text from Jeffrey. *I miss you.*

I find the pearl necklace he gave me and put it around my neck. I finger the pearls, remembering the afternoon in his bedroom where he kissed my entire body, starting at my toes, making his way up to the necklace.

I start to send him a reply: *I miss you, too. I miss your touch. The security I felt wrapped in your arms.* I delete that. *I want to fuck you,* I type and almost send. Isn't that as real as I get? The therapist would say those are only my surface feelings. What's real? *You're a sick old man,* I type. *I'm sixteen years old. Leave me alone.* But I delete that, too.

About the author:

Through college, Michelle spent her free time bartending and waiting tables. After completing her graduate degree at Cleveland State University, Michelle relocated to Phoenix to teach college-level English and literature courses. Today Michelle has found a new calling as a mother to her precious daughter.

Michelle's realistic fiction is inspired by her diverse experiences and the spirited people she has encountered along the way. She takes pride in being introspective and looking for the common humanity we all share, regardless of where we come from—the little things that connect us and have the power to inspire kindness and understanding.

"Pearl" is Michelle's most recent attempt to experiment with an unreliable narrator—show the reader a speaker who doesn't realize she is a victim, by default, in a fashion inspired by Nabokov's Lolita.

Michelle is honored to once again be published by Scribes Valley Publishing.

Michelle would like to thank her husband for his love and support.

TURTLE TREE
©2020 by Virginia M. Amis

"He's at it again."

Martin looked up from his easy chair, startled by Jill's intrusion into his Sunday golf-watching respite. "What?"

Jill motioned behind her with a quick twitch of her head. "George. He's at it again. The moment I sat down outside he started power-washing his back patio."

"You want me to kill him?" Martin asked, his eyes on the television screen.

Jill shook her head in frustration. "It's been going on for an hour! What is he cleaning? His patio's smaller than ours." She couldn't see through the vinyl fence, great for privacy, but sucky for spying on her neighbor. "It's friggin' Sunday! My day of rest!"

Martin pulled himself away from the golf game and took her in his arms. "I'll go get my gun," he whispered into her ear, the tickle of his breath making her squirm and laugh.

She felt a little better.

"Use your noise-canceling headphones," Martin offered, planting a kiss before he resumed vicariously playing the seventeenth hole of the Masters.

Jill closed the door to his refuge, mind spooling to find a solution that didn't involve headphones or murder. She settled on a walk through Wildwood Park. Leaving the house by the front door, she stopped to tie her shoe, realizing she didn't hear the power washer whining. Peering around the side of her house that bordered George Carter's, another irritation greeted her.

"Yip, yip, yip, yip." George's dog, ankle-biter Lucy, had lived next door to her and Martin for five years, and she still barked every time she saw one of them. "Yip, yip." Jiminy Christmas!

"Lucy! Stop!" George yelled. His bronzed face settled above his shirtless body, gray chest hair sparkling with water droplets, power washer wand in his dripping hand. The same script had played out for five years. Lucy barked and George yelled his shirtless ineffective warning. He shrugged at Jill. Lucy relieved herself in George's herb garden, where plants grew that Jill could not identify. Strange all around, she thought.

Jill gave George a weak wave and headed out for her walk. No use talking to him. Hadn't changed things in the past.

The back entrance to Wildwood Park branched off a gravel road only yards from their house. The road, shrouded in tall cedars and pines, looked more like a driveway than a public street hiding tucked-away houses and leading deep into the woods toward the Luckett Center for Mental Health. Jill and Martin walked this path all the time, always veering south into the park. They'd never ventured farther down the road. Signs pointed toward the community hospital's annex and they'd met strange-looking wanderers headed in that direction, carrying bags from Wal-Mart and vacant stares on their faces. Must be some good drugs used there, they'd joked.

Hopping over a trickle of water making a muddy stream, Jill stepped onto the park's paved road. Even the luxury of a dry clean path did not mar the feeling that she had entered a sanctuary. Towering on either side, skyscraper trees reached for the sun they blocked from her face. Big-ass maples, Martin called them, because their individual leaves were dinner-plate size. Firs and cedars accompanied them, spreading individual limbs in different shapes as they reached higher. Underneath, shorter vegetation scrambled for equal time. Laurels and rhododendrons elbowed each other for space. Forget-me-nots carpeted the forest floor, interspersed with stinging-nettles and salmon berry vines. Leaning snags and live trees, felled in the last wind storm which had knocked out Jill's power for three days, allowed for a little more light in some areas. As she walked the winding road, she grinned at the folly of some nature-lover who had hung suet feeders on the right-angled limbs of a dead tree, the large main trunk housing grey squirrels. It was a play house with free food. Wasn't the whole park the same thing?

A soft breeze had been blowing on this May afternoon, but the forest did not allow it to penetrate. A little warm, she tied her jacket around her waist and kept moving. Within twenty minutes, she'd forgotten about her neighbor's stupid antics.

The park gave the illusion it went on forever. Dirt paths snaked through the underbrush, purposely guiding a visitor to immerse, or become lost, in the woodland. Jill knew there was such a path ahead, just beyond the turtle tree. She and Martin had discovered it on a previous walk.

"Don't you think it looks like a turtle's head? Look—its head is covered with moss," she'd pointed toward the dead tree trunk beside the path the day she noticed it.

They were deep into the park that day. Martin had looked where she pointed. The snag rose fifty feet tall with a large protrusion on one side. "Huh," he'd said. "Maybe. I can make out a long snout and eye ridge, but..."

"Come on, you see it, don't you?" Jill had prodded.

He'd smiled. "Yeah, babe. I see it."

On her solitary walk today, she looked forward to seeing the forest creature, ready to greet an old friend. Edging around the bend, she spied it, without a doubt a turtle likeness protruding from the dead tree trunk. It made her smile. *Wonder what you would say if you could talk.*

Studying the tree, she felt her limbs relax, her heart rate slow. Gentle forest sounds accompanied her quieted thoughts. Moments passed. A dry leaf blew over her shoe. She breathed deeply, looking upward, accepting the gift, wishing Martin were there to share it. She stretched her arms out to her sides and closed her eyes, remaining in that pose until she heard voices from approaching walkers. She looked at the turtle head once more before pushing into the dense undergrowth, careful not to brush against the nettle.

Refreshed after an hour, Jill returned home. "What's this?" she said to no one as she spied a bottle of clear liquid resting on the door mat. The accompanying note read, *Hope you like anise liquor. Made it myself. George.*

Huh, Jill thought. A peace offering. Did little to replace her lost tranquility, but it counted for something. She hoped it hadn't originated in the herb garden she'd seen Lucy use as her toilet. Martin hated anise, so it would be all hers.

That night she tried a little in her coffee, hoping it would help her sleep. Martin shook his head. "How can you drink that stuff?"

Later, she felt like she was on fire. They made vigorous love and fell asleep. Before Jill noticed, the alarm played Mozart, annoying her into waking up.

"How'd you sleep?" Martin asked, leaning in for a kiss, his hair sticking out at all angles as though he'd had a fright.

Jill thought for a moment. "Really well. That stuff George gave me did the trick." She winked and Martin smiled.

After work that evening, Jill wanted to weed her strawberry garden. Wild geraniums loved the patch and tended to crowd the fruiting vines. It wasn't hard work and the evening air felt warm enough. Weeding always helped her decompress from a stressful work day. But, the moment she stepped outside, chaos reigned.

"*Yip, yip, yip!*"

"Lucy, stop!"

Jill tried to be quiet (in her own back yard!) but Lucy couldn't be fooled.

"*Yip, yip, yip, yip!*"

"Lucy, I said stop!"

This needed to end. Martin had a business meeting, wouldn't be home for hours. Jill had to take action on her own.

"Hey, George," she yelled over the fence, trying to keep the irritation level of her voice restrained. "Can you take Lucy inside? I plan to be out for the next thirty minutes."

Silence.

"George?"

A low grumbling came from the neighbor's patio. "She needs her fresh air. Can't you go inside?"

The nerve of him! Jill's work day had involved some grouchy clients and an assistant who failed to show. Weeding the strawberries had been her stress-relief plan. Apparently, George didn't agree. Lucy's needs came first.

Slamming the door to make her point, Jill went inside. Fuming, she brewed herself a cup of coffee. How dare he talk to her like that! As her brew finished, she spied the anise liquor sitting on the counter beside her mug. It took all she had to resist pouring it down the drain and smashing the glass container. Instead, she poured a long shot into her cup, consoling herself with large gulps until her blood pressure dropped. Her cell phone rang.

"Hey, Babe. How was your day?" Martin asked.

Jill intended to spare him George's antics, but spilled them in less than a minute, her anger fueling the trajectory.

"Whoa, Jill. Slow down. He's an old coot and that dog's all he has. He's a vet, remember? Combat and all that."

Jill rolled her eyes. George retired from the military twenty or more years ago. Something about his retirement story always left her with questions.

"Why don't you take a walk in Wildwood? I can't get out of this meeting, or I'd come home and beat him up for you."

Martin, her cool-headed hero. "Fine," Jill replied. "I'll take a walk."

Her shoes crunched along the gravel road. Dim light filtered through the tree tops, creating garish shadows. Jill didn't mind. The anise liquor had softened her edges. She'd donned her jacket as May evenings in the Northwest became cold quickly. Tugging it closer, she continued toward the cutoff leading to the park. Halfway down, a wild-eyed man jumped out of the underbrush.

"Jumped" might have been an exaggeration, Jill thought, as she tried to clear her head. But he did startle her.

"H-hey," she said in his direction, hoping her voice sounded friendly as she shifted her feet side to side, preparing to run.

He had hunched shoulders and a day's growth of beard on his young face. Twenty-two, twenty-three? she guessed. He lifted hooded eyes toward her and said nothing. Thick, chapped lips, she noticed. Protruding from his coat sleeves were large hands, the largest hands she'd ever seen, even on her grandfather who towered over her at six-five. This guy was only five-ten, but his hands could have wrapped around her neck and had length to spare. One hand reached into his pocket. Jill tensed. A gun? Knife? Did they let the mental patients have weapons?

When his hand reappeared, he held two pieces of wrapped candy. Taffy, she thought, the kind shops sold near the beach. Is that how the hospital gave its mental patients drugs? she wondered. Jill watched him unwrap a piece and chew it slowly. He held out the second one to her.

She shook her head. "Thanks, no."

"It's okay. Just taffy. Not crazy drugs." A smile crept across his face, making him a little less scary. He must have heard the gossip.

Afraid to say no, Jill took it, depositing it into her pocket. "Thanks. See you."

She took off into the park, turning every so many yards to see if he was following her, reaching the turtle tree before she realized she'd walked that far. Suddenly tired, she rested with her back against the snag's smooth trunk. Her nose began to run.

From her pocket, she pulled a tissue. The taffy fell to the ground. Wiping the tissue across her nose, she stuffed it back into her pocket and picked up the taffy.

Martin would not be happy about her encounters tonight. He tried to stay friendly with neighbors, but had her back first. George's rudeness couldn't be excused, she heard in her head. And, he would not like it if she told him she'd run into a mental health patient who offered her candy, less so if he found out she'd taken it.

The shrubs behind the turtle tree rustled, startling her. A chill ran through her veins, raising her alertness. Madman? Squirrel, she hoped, scanning the landscape. The movement stopped. Jill sighed, chiding herself for being alarmed. She'd never heard of any attacks by animals or humans in the park. She was being childish.

As her heart resumed its normal cadence, Jill's head began to spin. She heard her stomach growling. Crap! She'd had alcohol on an empty stomach.

The taffy lay in her palm. Innocuous-looking in white opaque paper, she didn't see any puncture wounds. A needle inserting a "secret" filling leaves a mark. No mark, at least on the outside. Probably fine. Her head continued spinning. She needed something to soak up the alcohol, tide her over until she could eat dinner. Otherwise, she would not have considered it.

She unwrapped the candy and didn't see anything strange. Pressing it with her fingers, nothing squished out. She took a small bite, tasting its sweetness. *Hell with it*, she thought. The whole piece went into her mouth.

Chewing slowly, the flavor reminded her of a trip to Ocean Shores with Martin. He'd laughed at her when she ate piece after piece, enjoying the soft chewy goodness, twisting the empty wrappers and tossing them into the trash.

The dizziness she'd felt a minute ago seemed better, but now Jill felt exhausted. Her back against the turtle tree, she yearned to sleep. She let herself slip down to a sitting position.

"Closing my eyes for just a minute," she murmured.

She woke with a start at the sound of a voice.

"What are you doing?" His voice was neither threatening nor comforting.

She looked around. The sun had set on the park, long shadows giving way to complete darkness. Chilled to the bone, she tried to stand up, but her legs wouldn't hold her. She heard the voice again.

"Hey! Wake up. What are you doing? You shouldn't be here in the woods. It's nighttime. You need to go home."

Jill couldn't focus her eyes in the dark. The voice seemed nearby. She shook, unable to control her body temperature.

"I'm the turtle," the voice said with a chuckle, as though pleased with himself.

Where was she? She tried to remember. The walk. Candy. Turtle tree. She leaned her head back and looked up.

The voice spoke to her again with more urgency. "Go home. That way."

Jill didn't care if the turtle tree was taking to her. She needed help. Every way she looked darkness swallowed the path. *Going mad*, she thought. *Talking tree!*

"What way?" she said, her voice coming out as a whisper. The ground began to crawl. Jill pulled her knees toward her chest, kicking at the moving creatures, yelling at them to get back, brushing them furiously off her legs, only to have more crawl on her arms. Nettles stung her skin.

A whistling noise split her ear drums. The voice called out, "Over here. At the turtle tree." The bushes rustled again, and the voice stopped.

Footsteps pounded, hurting her head. She covered her face as hands grabbed her, calling out her name.

Later, her fingers wrapped around a hot mug of coffee, shoulders draped in her mother's afghan, she watched from the living room sofa as Martin talked to the police officers around the kitchen island.

"Has she ever had one of these episodes before?" an officer named C. Pruitt asked.

Martin shook his head. "Never. I don't know what happened. The paramedics didn't find any head injuries. Only this wrapper in her pocket." His hand held the white opaque taffy wrapper.

Did he drug her, the crazy man she met in the woods? Jill sat silently trying to remember.

Officer Pruitt took the wrapper, placing it in an evidence bag. "Just in case," he said. Turning to leave, he asked if he could speak with Jill again, thinking she hadn't been coherent when they'd found her in the woods.

As he took a step towards her, the back door opened and a short, chunky officer came inside the kitchen. Lucy's barking pierced the night air. Jill covered her ears. Martin shook his head.

"That damn dog," he said. "Our neighbor can't control him. Drives us nuts." It was out before he realized what he'd said. "Sorry, babe."

Jill looked at him. Did he think she was nuts? Was she the next resident of the mental health facility in the woods?

"Who's your neighbor?" Officer Pruitt asked.

"George Carver," Martin answered. "Lives there with his dog."

"George Carver?" he repeated, exchanging a look with his partner.

Jill wanted to speak, to convince the officers her mind had returned to normal. "He's a jerk of a neighbor. Uses his power-washer for hours on end, then lets his dog bark at us as though we were strangers. Really annoying. I wish you could arrest him."

No one laughed. "Did he used to be in the military?" Pruitt asked.

Jill nodded. "That's what he told us. Guess he doesn't have anyone but that stupid dog for company. And," she stood, dragging the afghan with her, "he grows herbs and makes his own booze. He gave me this bottle of anise liquor," she indicated toward the bottle on the counter. "Left it on the front door step yesterday. I took it as an apology for irritating the hell out of us."

"Anise liquor?" The short officer shot a glance toward his partner. "Did you drink any?"

Jill sat down on a bar stool; her legs still wobbly. "Yeah, I've had a few shots in my coffee."

Officer Pruitt eyed the bottle, raised his eyebrows and handed it to his partner. After a huddle, they asked if they could take the bottle with them for testing.

Jill looked at Martin. "Testing for what?"

Martin and Jill appreciated the quiet in their back yard. Sitting in patio chairs, they enjoyed the late afternoon. No need to keep their voices low now that George and Lucy were gone. Jill felt only a slight sense of sadness when the officers led George out of his front door in hand cuffs, wearing nothing more than shorts and canvas shoes. Lucy had gone to a relative, one who would care for her while George faced charges of lacing his anise liquor with speed and ground sleeping pills. They told Jill she might have some residual effects, hallucinations and flashbacks, but none had happened so far. Probably because she'd only had a few shots of the liquor.

George confessed to drugging her. He didn't appreciate Jill's complaints about Lucy's barking. He wanted Jill to succumb to the drugs, act crazy, maybe be committed to the mental health hospital with his grandson, who had lived with him before Martin and Jill moved to the neighborhood. They heard he'd repeatedly stolen from George, angering him into a frenzy. The police knew his grandson from many run-ins with the law, and had last picked him up for driving high and crashing his vehicle into a parked car. George helped the prosecutor's case, testifying against his grandson at trial. The court released the young man from prison after three years, with the arrangement that he go to Luckett Center for treatment. George went to see him there, but his grandson showed no improvement, the officers told Jill. Until now, when George could no longer visit.

His grandson, Patrick, had been ranting to the police for years, claiming his grandfather was drugging him with the treats he insisted on bringing him, made with natural ingredients from George's garden. Laced with poison, Patrick claimed. The police ignored him. Eat them, the nurses encouraged the weakened, lonely young man, convincing him that his grandfather must care for him deeply to go to such effort. Besides, no one else ever visited. Beaten down and lonely, Patrick ate what his grandfather gave him, sinking deeper into himself. Now and then, he stole saltwater taffy from one of the nurses and went for a walk, learning Wildwood Park's trails like the back of his large hands.

Jill had met the young madman when he offered her some taffy. He'd saved her from freezing to death that night at the turtle tree. Roused her. Tried to coax her home. Kept her safe until Martin found her. Whistled loudly when they were close.

Martin's hand found hers. "Want to go for a walk?"

They ventured down the gravel lane, this time passing the park entrance and walking to the Luckett Center, a bag of taffy in Jill's pocket. In the clearing, Patrick sat in a vinyl chair on the facility's porch, eyes bright, waving as they approached. He'd be released soon, the drugs working themselves out of his system and the therapy he received helping him make positive strides toward independence. Their friendship had grown over the last several months. They would miss him.

Patrick had saved Jill from the real madman. Maybe, they'd saved each other.

About the author:

Virginia Amis is a lawyer and a writer, who spends her days in a courtroom and her nights and weekends writing fiction. A transplant from Pittsburgh to the Pacific Northwest, she writes in that setting, bringing nature and characters to life through her stories. She has written two fiction novels and has a third in progress. Her short stories have been published in *Reminisce Extra*, *Perspectives Magazine*, Scribes Valley 2019 anthology *Beyond the Norm*, and *101words.com*.

SERVED COLD
©2020 by Joseph J. Salerno

The young man and the older woman walked side by side past a gallery filled with priceless paintings and into a large, naturally lit, glass-enclosed hall. They continued to walk slowly down the middle of the hall and gazed at the few dozen or so life-sized statues on each side of them. It was The Garden of Statues at The Metropolitan Museum of Art in New York. He had recently been in the hall a few times; she hadn't seen it in many years. He promised her refreshment, as he knew that at the far end of the imposing sculptures there was a small vending kiosk with cold drinks.

"Seltzer?" he asked.

"Yes, thank you. With ice and lemon, if available."

They sat on a bench near the small and tidy kiosk, she with her seltzer and he with a cold Pepsi.

"Do you remember ever having been in this place, this Garden of Statues?"

"Vaguely," she responded. "Very vaguely, and quite a long time ago. But it is beautiful. I just wonder, why the dim lighting?"

The sun had not yet set behind the glass-paned walls. The small spotlights at the base of the sculptures were not yet turned on. It was a bit eerie and dark.

"Effect, I suppose," he simply said. "Effect."

He walked a few paces back to the last of the large statues on the side of the aisle. Count Ugolino and His Sons. It was a gruesome life-sized piece of marble on a pedestal, an old man in agony clutching onto four starving children around and beneath him.

"Mother," he said in a slightly raised voice, "Meet Count Ugolino and his sons."

From the small bench near the refreshment stand, the woman turned to see her son point to the large piece of marble. She remained seated, though slightly hunched over, raised her plastic cup and said, "Nice to meet you, Count. Count Ugo—?"

"Count Ugolino and his starving sons!"

She admired her son's own statuesque form pointing to the marble. He reminded her of her late husband, same figure, same look, and a flair for the melodramatic. He would become a great legal scholar and orator.

"And why," she began to ask, clearing her throat with a sip of seltzer, "why are they all starving?"

He had walked with her that late afternoon for hours, waiting for her to ask that very question. Past dozens of rooms of priceless art to have her there—*there*—at Count Ugolino's feet, where she would naively ask, "Why are they all starving?"

"In truth, they are not all starving," he said. "I will relate the story in a nutshell. Ugolino was a powerful Count in old Italy, circa 1288, and his political enemies took over his little city-state of Pisa and put him and his kids behind bars. While in prison, his captors gave him and his children very little food, essentially only enough for one person. The family, father and sons, decided to keep only the father alive, in hopes that one day he would be able to get out and exact revenge on his enemies. The children died in prison and so, eventually, did the Count. Ugolino never got his revenge." The young man took a sip of his Pepsi. "Anyway, at this point in the story, Mother, they are not all starving."

As the sun started to set on the glass-enclosed "garden," small lights began to dimly glow in front of each statue. The woman wiped her brow with her fingers and sipped her seltzer.

"That is a terrible story," she said, "and quite an ugly sculpture. I mean *ugly*. Look at those wretched children. And what is the Count doing there, biting his fingernails?"

"I did not say it was pretty, but the story is based in truth. And being based in truth, it might be, well, true."

"It is what it is, it is true because it is true," she mocked. "You spent four years at Columbia to learn these brilliant platitudes?"

"No," he replied, touching the base of the statue, on which was engraved the sculptor's name, Jean-Baptiste Carpeaux, and the date of the carving, 1865-67. "I didn't go there to learn platitudes. I did go there to learn that I don't need to feed my parents, feed the dead, feed the past. There will be no law school in my future, Mother."

She smiled a nervous smile and took a sip of her seltzer. "What are you talking about? That's all we've planned for you your whole life. Debate teams, student councils. Your father would be very disappointed to hear you talking right now, Peter."

She sat there about twelve feet away and watched him slowly walk around the statue. He was pensive, as if having some sort of revelation, looking at the thing while stroking his chin. He stood in awe in front of the large piece and pointed up to it. Again, she thought, he was being a bit melodramatic.

"They say, vengeance is a dish that is best served cold. What do you think of that statement? Do you believe it, Mother?"

"I'm not sure what you are referring to. My dear Peter, all this— emotion—over this statue, this Ugolino fellow. I mean, come on!"

"I'm going to Arizona to try to earn an MFA in Creative Writing. I'll be working as an assistant copy editor for a small newspaper in Phoenix. No law school, no bar exam, no future partnership in Dad's old firm."

"Vengeance," she whispered. "Is that what this is about?" She put some of the ice from her cup in a few napkins and placed the wad on her left knee. Her arthritis was acting up again, but her pain at her son's anger was greater. The words "assistant copy editor" echoed and clanged in her ears.

"You walk with me through The Met for two hours, and we end up here at sunset with this Count Ugolino, where you decide to tell me this, this—what? The kitchen or the den at home would not do? Why here, in front of this ugly statue?"

Peter looked at the sculpture and thought, Yes, it is ugly. Old man biting his fingers, four scrawny sons in agony at his sides and feet. Starvation, yielding to elders, death. He knew he had brought his mother here for a reason, but despite his penchant for drama, he wanted it to be more like cold water to the face than a dagger to the heart.

"Mrs. Haughwout, have I been a dutiful son?"

She shot him an angry glare. "Oh, it's 'Mrs. Haughwout' now. For twenty-two years it's been 'Mom' or 'Mother,' but now it's 'Mrs. Haughwout!'" She sighed. "Yes, Peter, you've been a very dutiful son."

"Well, it might be time to be something else. I do believe that diving into legal texts for years and becoming like my father," he again pointed to the Count, "I believe it would be kinda, like *that*! A starvation would set in. I myself would be biting my fingernails, or yielding like those dying sons. I would feel imprisoned. Hell, I already feel imprisoned. How much more graphic can I be?"

Mrs. Haughwout ordered another seltzer with ice and lemon from the bow-tied gentleman at the kiosk. Once again, she sat on the bench about twelve feet from Ugolino and put some ice on her arthritic knee. The sun had now completely set on The Garden of Statues, and each sculpture was softly and directly illumined by a small light near its base. It was a lovely but sad display, made more sad by her son's description of his life as an "imprisonment." She wasn't totally buying it.

"You know, Peter," she finally said. "There is this thing called the Internet. You simply could have Googled the image of this thing and shown it to me. It would have spared me some knee pain."

"Sorry, I almost forgot about your knees. I'm also sorry for getting so graphic, so *melodramatic*, as you like to say. But no, that's not true. I actually meant to be just that."

"Are we finished here?" she asked. "These poor people starved about seven hundred and thirty years ago. We are not much help to them now. Shall we go?"

She got up and prepared to walk out with him. As she passed the statue and touched its base, she said, "Thank you, Count. I'm sorry for your fate, but thank you for allowing my son to express his feelings. You have been an excellent, uh, conduit. As we get home, I hope that my son and I can discuss this matter a bit further."

"There is really nothing left to discuss," said Peter, as he took her by the arm and they began to walk away.

"We'll see."

About the author:

I was born and raised in Brooklyn, New York. A product of twelve years of Catholic school and three years at Columbia, I took a rather long time to "find myself." Once having been "found," I've spent the past twenty-six years as the Office Manager of a small tax accounting firm. I enjoy doing crossword puzzles and cooking, but I warn against doing both simultaneously.

I have self-published eleven chapbooks of short stories in the last seven years. It is always my aim to write densely-packed prose conveying ambiguity, metaphor, and multi-layered meaning. That is what I enjoy reading, so that is what I enjoy writing.

I have a Bachelor of Arts Degree in Psychology from SUNY, Empire State College. I live in a small apartment, along with about a dozen large house plants, three blocks from the New York City limits. I find foliage to be soothing, and I am a big admirer of oxygen.

PEE JA
©2020 by Bill Frank Robinson

The desert heat does not forgive error and I did not have trail experience with Pee Ja, the cold weather dog. In addition, she was female, a complication I didn't fully appreciate.

I hear fireworks blasting from across the road. Damn! It's two weeks until the Fourth of July. I grab my five-foot-long walking stick (some call it a club, throw the door open, and charge out into the back yard. Whoa! Just before I drop my foot across the threshold, I see a pile of black and white fur trembling on the stoop. I adjust and leap beyond the pile but now I'm out of control. My boot slides off the concrete steps and I sit down hard. "Ow!" I scream as I turn to confront my nemesis. Pee Ja is cowering, shaking, and pressing her body against my house. Her eyes are apologetic, pitiful. I can't blame her. She has good reason to fear the firecrackers, cherry bombs, and rockets because she lives with the perpetrators of this insult to the ear and mind.

"Pee Ja, my little baby." I wrap my arm around her and drag her into my lap where we exchange hugs and kisses. "Did those big mean boys chase you away from home?" Pee Ja is all over me now, bathing my face with a slobbery tongue. With more than a little effort I wrestle her down and hold her head under my arm. "There, there, calm down everything is going to be all right." She gradually calms and we talk. The talk turns into a debate; what are we going to do about the noise and the noisemakers? My initial response is out of the question with Pee Ja involved: she would never side with me against her family. (One day a football bounced across the road and I retrieved it. I motioned the boy chasing it to run out for a pass. I dropped a perfect spiral over his left shoulder and into his waiting hands. My joy was short-lived. There was a snarl, tearing of leg and Levi's, and a howl of pain from me. Pee Ja was letting me know that she does not tolerate anybody, even her best friend, to throw missiles at one of her family. I chased her and she hid out for a week.)

We could call the sheriff but he is at least forty miles away and probably busy. The law isn't a good idea anyway: my neighbors would never forgive me. "Well, Pee Ja, we're going to have to saddle up Old Blue and get outta town. She's hopping for joy as she bounces toward my rusty old blue pickup. I hook the battery cable up, climb into the cab (Pee Ja scurries across my lap and settles into the passenger seat), fire the engine, and head toward Pa Ha Road. I turn onto the roadway just as a string of firecrackers explode. We don't care, we're not going to be around. Old Blue heads for the highway one mile away.

"Pee Ja, look there. That's the Mexican Trailers." She stands up with both front paws on the dashboard, sweating with her tongue, and wagging her tail. The Mexican Trailers are the only dwellings between my house and the highway. I never called them that until I saw the work order for the technician that hooked up my TV cable. His directions to my house read: *½ mile past the Mexican trailers*. The Mexicans must have moved away before I was born because that cluster of rusted out old trailer homes have been vacant as long as I can remember. Wait! Just a minute. There is someone that lives in those trailers. An old woman, a hermit, lives there. She's crazy. I can hear her cackling when the wind's just right, raises the hair on the back of my neck. I walk past her on the road sometimes. She wears a shabby long black coat, flowery long dress (I can see a union suit below the dress), man's high-top shoes, and a shapeless hat. Her clothes are old-fashioned and too warm for the hot weather. I say, "Hi" and she looks right through me and never looks back as she walks away. Nobody knows where that white woman comes from or how she gets her food.

We come to the end of Pa Ha and turn right onto the main road. "Pee Ja, this is Highway 168." I'm trying to get her to laugh but she doesn't understand the joke. There's no reason why she should because she's not privy to the talk about 168. This thoroughfare is no thoroughfare; it just goes up in the mountains and ends. A truck driver from Texas drove his loaded rig up there. He was looking for a shortcut to San Francisco. What he found was a boulder that his truck hung up on when he tried to turn around. They had to bring a crane all the way from Los Angeles to get him back to the highway. One night a guy car-jacked a vehicle in town, drove out 168 at one hundred miles an hour with the sheriff and Highway Patrol close behind. He abandoned the car in deep snow, and ran into the mountains. A tow truck hauled the stolen property back to town and the law officers went home, had dinner, and went to bed. Early the next morning the sheriff drove up 168 and arrested the fugitive as he staggered down the hill. The lawyer told the court that his client was not very sophisticated.

There isn't much to see as you drive up 168, most all the rocks, sagebrush, and hills look alike and not a tree anywhere. The road is steep and straight as an arrow as it points to the great mountains. Ten miles up the road we encounter one large red mesa-like formation. "Hey, Pee Ja look over there. That's Red Hill. That's where all the outlaw Indians live. There aren't many of that Red Hill bunch left. They're the ones who refused to come on the reservation back in 1939."

Old Blue is chugging now; she doesn't like to go uphill.

"You think we gone far enough now, Pee Ja? Old Blue don't sound like she's in for the long haul." She wags her tail and jumps around the cab barking. We turn onto the pole line road and drive off the highway a quarter of a mile or so, park and get out.

I watch as Pee Ja scampers down the side of the ravine and splashes in the creek. This creek is usually dry but today, for some unknown reason, the water is running briskly. Pee Ja is aptly named "The Bear," with her long black fur and roly-poly body. She's sensitive, too, barking and leaping and snapping at my face, trying to shut me up, while I repeat my favorite tease; "My little chubby butt. My little chubby butt."

Jehrue, the old Basque sheepherder, told me that one must be careful with female dogs because, unlike the males, they will follow you till they die. I know that Rowdy, Pee Ja's predecessor, would leave me and return to the truck if I traveled beyond his capabilities. I always found him lying under the truck when I returned from my walks. So how do I protect Pee Ja with her long hair and female properties? I'll follow the creek; the cold water will relieve any heat exhaustion.

From up here, high on the hill, I can see the whole mostly barren valley. Running the length of the valley is the Owen's River; I can't see the water, but trees and dense greenery mark its course. To the north there's Laws, the old ghost town; there's a railroad museum there now. All I can see from up here is a cluster of buildings and a giant cottonwood. The narrow-gage railroad tracks ran from Carson City to Los Angeles. Then they shut her down (the train was called the "Slim Princess") and tore the tracks out. We could use that railroad today.

South of Laws I can see the large airport hangar and west of the airport the trees where town is but I can't see the houses; it's hard to believe that three thousand people live under that cluster of trees. Across the valley are the White Mountains where the bristle cone pines grow—the oldest living things in the World. The most famous bristle cone, Methuselah, is 6,000 years old. His location is not marked to protect him from souvenir hunters.

"Get him, Pee Ja! Get him!" I am laughing and shouting as Pee Ja chases a rabbit. She's running south as the rabbit has circled through the brush and is fleeing to the north. His body flashes in and out of sight but Pee Ja is looking in the opposite direction. I cover my mouth so not to call her a dumbbell. She leaps on a boulder and, from that vantage point, can look over the tops of the bushes but she's still looking the wrong way; she'll never catch that rabbit.

Once, Rowdy flushed a coyote out of the same creek. I ran after them as hard as I could with my stick in both hands: stories have been told of coyotes luring dogs into the brush, pouncing on them, and having them for supper. Fortunately, Rowdy never caught the coyote and maybe saved us both. The tales were of one coyote leading the dog to a pack of coyotes but I never saw coyotes in packs. When I see them, they are always traveling alone except one time, up by the White Mountains, I did see two running together. I figured they were mating.

Damn! The day is almost gone. Pee Ja and I have been so engrossed with our trip we have traveled farther than we intended. The sheepherder was right: Pee Ja, except for occasional rabbit chases, has stayed right with me. And she has shown no sign of weakening from the heat. Of course, I have halted every ten minutes or so and allowed her to play in the water. But now we need to get to the truck before dark; when the sun disappears behind the mountains it will be freezing. I'm not dressed for the cold and I won't be able to find my way in the dark. It took us seven hours following the creek but that creek meanders. If we go back in a straight line, cross-country, we can make it in less than two hours. I fill my water jug, grab my stick and march away from the stream. Pee Ja follows.

I have been jogging up the hill for twenty minutes and I am going to beat that sun with plenty of time to spare. The heat is relentless and much hotter without the cooling effects of the running water, but I feel good. I look back for Pee Ja and she has disappeared. I call her name and there is no answer. I retrace my steps and twenty yards back I find her lying in the scant shade of a small rock. "Pee Ja, get up." I grab her and pull her to her feet. She sags and keels over as I try to hold her up. It's like all her resources are being used to pant. "Pee Ja, how about a little water?" I unscrew the jug lid and pour water into it. I hold the makeshift vessel under her nose and she drinks greedily. I keep feeding her water and trying to get her on her feet. She consumes all the precious liquid and is still unable to stand. I look back the way we have come; the creek is downhill and the closest but if I carry her there, we will have to spend the night and what if she don't recover? I can't leave her and go for the truck because I might never be able to find her again. I've got to get help for her: she could be dying. I throw the empty jug and my prized, exquisitely carved eighty-dollar walking stick into the brush. I'll probably never see it again.

"Come on, Pee Ja. Try to help me." I get on my knees and push my hands under her and scoop her up onto my chest. I cradle her in my arms and stagger to my feet. She must weigh eighty pounds and she's limp; it's like carrying a butchered hog.

I head straight up the hill, straight towards the truck. The going is slow, laborious; I have to keep using my knee to push the limp Pee Ja back up into my arms. I can't maintain a straight line; I'm staggering like a drunken man. Pee Ja's head is slumped over; she's barely breathing. I am trying to go faster and can't. They say when people overheat the brain stops working properly: they get confused and travel in circles until they collapse. That can't happen to me because I only got one direction to go—uphill.

I'm still trucking—it seems like forever. I don't look up anymore. I look down at the ground and count steps, one, two, three.... When I get up into the sixties or so I lose count and start over. I know the sun's still above the mountains but I don't know how far above it is; I don't want to know. My back is throbbing and my left side has a cramp. My arms are dead. I need to rest but if I lay Pee Ja down, I may never be able to get her up again. I feel dizzy but that's normal in the hot sun.

I walk into cool shade, thank God. I look up and I am next to a giant rock. A giant rock? There isn't any big rock between the truck and me. Where am I? I look around and see my truck far below me. I have walked a half-mile past Old Blue!

I lay my burden down in the shade and lean against the rock to rest my arms and back. She doesn't move or open her eyes but she's still breathing. I can get back down the hill in ten minutes but how can I get the truck up here? It looks like the faint outline of an old road just south of me; I can drive as close as possible to Pee Ja and carry her to my vehicle.

I look back at Pee Ja. She's not moving, and I'll be back within thirty minutes, so I race for the truck. It's a relief to go downhill and I'm soon opening the door and climbing in. I turn the key and get a slow grind. Damn! I didn't unhook the battery cable; my battery has lost its charge. I leap to the ground and push but Old Blue ain't pushing. I grab my shovel from the bed and start shoveling dirt from the back of the rear tires. I finish my undermining operation, throw my tool into the truck bed, race to the front bumper, and start pushing. Old Blue lunges backwards and begins rolling downhill, picking up speed as she goes. I race after her and swing aboard just as we crash into a rock and come to a stop. I check things out and the rock is all that's holding my truck on this steep section. I get my car jack, wedge it under the front tire, and tie a rope to the jack. I shove the rope end through the driver's side window, grab my shovel and start digging the rock out of the ground. I free the rock and use the shovel handle to roll it out of the way. Old Blue shutters and the tires on the right side roll a couple of inches but the jack and brakes hold. I climb into the cab, throw in the clutch, shift into reverse, release the brakes, and pull on the rope. The jack flies from under the tire and we jump backwards. I push on the gas, release the clutch, and the engine roars to life. I brake to a stop, engage the clutch, and slam the gears into granny-low. The vehicle groans and shakes when I depress the gas pedal and let go of the clutch but she climbs slowly up the hill.

I'm only fifty feet from where I left Pee Ja when I decide to turn around and point towards Highway 168. I leave the engine running and wedge rocks under the wheels to help the brakes. I run to grab my unconscious friend but she's not there. She's not where I left her! "Pee Ja! Pee Ja!" I shout but I get no answer. I run in circles, calling her name. Thirty yards downhill I find her. She must of woke up and followed me only to collapse again.

I'm racing down 168 with Pee Ja lying on the seat beside me. She's not moving. I've killed that dog. It's getting dark when I roar into my neighbor's yard honking my horn. Kyle and Chase meet me in the yard. "It's Pee Ja. She got overheated. You got to take her to the vet. I'm feeling sick myself." The two boys pull her out of the truck. "Can you get her to the vet?" Kyle, the college student home for the summer, nods yes. I spin Old Blue around and drive for home.

I wake with a headache and fierce thirst. I stagger into the kitchen and drink water. My calendar watch says it's been four days since my adventure with Pee Ja. I've been sick and out of my head for most of the time. How is Pee Ja? Is she alive? I leave my cool, dark house and walk out into the hot sun. I call her name and don't get a response. I go back inside, dress, and walk out into the back yard and around the house towards Pa Ha Road. I can hear the loud music as I approach Pee Ja's house. I enter the yard and still no Pee Ja bouncing to greet me. Kyle is sitting under the large shade trees. There is a pitcher of lemonade and booming stereo on the table beside him.

I shout, "Where is Pee Ja?" He looks at me, puzzled. He turns the stereo down and I repeat my question.

"She went to town with Mom."

"She's OK then. Was she very sick?"

Kyle breaks into a big grin. "Are you kidding? Twenty minutes after you left her here, she was running around the yard looking for trouble."

About the author:

Born while traveling on the road in Raton, New Mexico, April 4th, 1932. My dad was a road builder or "Grading Contractor" as his business card identified him. Consequently, my early schooling was a series of one room country school houses scattered amongst the states of Colorado, Wyoming, New Mexico, and Texas.

In 1938 the Great Depression closed down our company and the sheriff auctioned all our trucks, steam shovels and bull dozer tractors. Dad hopped a freight train for California while Mom and I hitch-hiked to Denver to live with her sister. Later we joined the great migration to California.

WWII gave the Robinson family a few years of prosperity as we started a chicken ranch to take advantage of meat shortages caused by the war-time economy. The war ended and we went bankrupt causing the Robinsons to scatter. I followed the harvests and traveled to Idaho to work in the mines but I was too young so I worked odd jobs until I was seventeen and could join the military. While in basic training the Korean War broke out and I soon found myself in Korea.

Discharged from the military I went to work in Los Angeles, married, and raised a family.

I retired in 1987 and moved to my wife's hometown where I have been working at the craft of writing stories. My fictional stories of Archie Cleebo based on my growing up experiences have gotten good reviews and have been published by a woman who lives in Ireland. My hope is to put all my short stories together and publish a book entitled "Archie Cleebo."

ONE WAY
©2020 by Bear Kosik

The cellphone was useless here. It needed a charge anyway. All around the uniformity of the landscape was matched by the uniformity of the overcast sky. Yes, in one direction—west?—some trees marked the horizon and in the opposite the less dark line of a ridge. Or maybe they were both ridges. Hard to tell. There's rarely a need to reach an accurate conclusion in situations like this. Then again, accuracy itself is usually a moving target in situations like this.

The blacktop intersecting horizontally with his path snaked into those distances. Maybe snaked isn't the right word for a road that offers a classic example of foreshortened visual perspective. Nature has been known to create things that appear perfectly linear, but only human engineering can pull this off. See the problem with trying to be accurate? Maybe that's why straightforward isn't actually a direction.

What sounded like a chainsaw could be heard. It was impossible to tell where it was coming from. Certainly not from behind him, unless.... This had been happening more often than usual lately. Two possible paths, no bars, not much juice left anyway, and nobody left to blame. No wonder Janus is known for looking both ways and never crossing.

Somewhere somebody had to have a schedule that listed exactly how many wrong turns someone can take in life before everything was required to smooth itself out. Those wrong turns certainly seemed to have been piling up. Sure, it came with the territory when you live life off the straight and narrow. But Delmont Thomas thought he had corrected his ways sufficiently to no longer expect every choice he made was most likely going to be a bad one.

He knew it couldn't have always been like this. There had to be a turning point when he veered off from the trajectory set up by elders, environment, and early education. That's right. Go all the way back to...what? The decision not to go to college? Hell! That was probably the right way to go. Who knew?

The problem when Delmont Thomas had a choice to make was that he couldn't tell if it was a right choice or a good choice even long after it had been made. What did that therapist tell him? You make the best choice you can at the time given the information you have at that time. Maybe it sounded more profound then because he always went to therapy appointments stoned. The giggles from being high certainly kept away any diagnosis of depression.

The trouble is that way of thinking assumes a person is seriously considering the situation and the options available every time a choice needs to be made. It doesn't take into account whether the person is intelligent enough to understand the facts or diligent enough to look into the facts. It assumes people actually care enough to put some positive effort into the task of deciding all of those things in life that need to be decided. It helps to be clean and sober, too.

That was a condition Delmont Thomas had acquired after much whining and conniving due to the way addictions repurpose good intentions to achieve instant gratification. It wasn't a coincidence that the forty-three-year-old still clung more firmly to a large book of Escher drawings with their impossible stairways than the Big Book of Alcoholics Anonymous. Staying stopped when it came to drugs and alcohol required finding the exit, something in those illustrations that Delmont was determined to find. All the Big Book provided was a roadmap to progress once one found an exit.

Ariana Delgado gave the Escher book to Delmont twenty-two years before. She gave him his first Big Book twelve years later. At no point did she ever question whether she had done those two tasks in the correct order. That was one of her finest qualities in Delmont Thomas' eyes.

She was, and remained, the closest thing to a steady fuck he had in this lifetime. That was her word by the way. For years, Ariana was home base or maybe the pole Delmont's balls were tethered to when he started flying around. It sure seemed like he was going in circles every time he ventured out looking for...what?

Maybe that was the problem. Behind every decision lies a goal. Sometimes it is unstated. Sometimes it is unachievable. Nonetheless, a purpose, a next thing stands on the path one chooses. The choice is made in order to reach that goal.

But Delmont Thomas lacked goals. He prided himself on not thinking much of the future, not dwelling on dreams when things needed to be done here and now. Turning down that baseball scholarship reflected his embrace of the present. Why chase hopes of getting into the Majors or earning the first degree anyone had in his family? As far as Delmont Thomas was concerned, the future did not exist.

Any choice Delmont made was missing a goal to focus on once the choice was made. He could find all the reasons he needed not to do things. Whittled down in that manner, the options ended with something he could find no reason not to do. So, that's what he would do. Simple.

That's how he and Ariana stayed more or less together for so long. There was never a reason to give up the security of a safe house to crash at tended by a beautiful soul with a comforting body. Even when she got married, the light remained on. Only she could find a wife who understood how some relationships could not be altered by a vow of commitment made later in the game.

Ariana was the reason he was at this point in his life not knowing which direction to head. He was compelled to find some other means of comforting his ego enough to not depend on a married lover to do so. Maybe he was gaining a sense of dignity that now prevented him from insinuating himself into someone's relationship based on seniority. But where had that left him? Facing two different ways to go, with a dead battery and no bars, and nobody he could reasonably blame.

Three hours earlier, Delmont had turned off whatever road he was on to check out a place claiming to be an opal mine where folks could dig up their own gemstones. He liked opals in the same way he liked raspberries, not in the same way he liked cats. They always attracted his attention, but he could live without them.

That reminded him. Once he did have a working phone again, he'd better check whether Junior was going in and feeding the cats or just leaving a bag of kibble on the floor for them to tear into. At least he knew they had access to water so long as that Buddha fountain in the den kept running. Come to think of it, Ariana gave him that too, completely from concern about the cats living with a human who tended to go feral than any thought of Delmont's spiritual needs.

With no more information than a weary sign saying, *Dig for Opals Mine Open to Public*, Delmont was on his way. The trek down to the site was an hour-long gut-buster. Either the mine was not productive enough for the owners to provide pavement or they found more productive ways of using the money made from the mine.

The place looked exactly like one might expect an old mine to look like somewhere around the Oregon-Nevada border. A family of four from Minnesota was finishing up their adventure. Aside from looking dusty and sweaty, they seemed cheerful enough. Then again, Delmont suspected everyone from Minnesota was required to be cheerful all the time or face banishment to North Dakota.

The mine operator turned out to be on the young side of geezer, just the kind of guy you did not want to look at if he was standing next to you at a urinal unless you were really that desperate. Flat fee of sixty-two genuine American dollars got a person a ten-pound sack of rock to pummel in the hopes of finding some milky opalescence within.

Unlike the times when one has reached a fork in the road and must choose left or right, making the decision to spend money always has a lot more considerations to consider. Someone in Mr.

Thomas' socioeconomic demographic had to weigh the probabilities of finding something of value and the pleasures of whacking at stones for half an hour or so against the priorities of gas, food, and lodging once this detour was in the rearview mirror. Added in was the time spent having already made the turn. What does one do in this situation?

As foretold, victory comes to the choice that requires the least amount of activity. Delmont looked around the place a bit, ignoring the proprietor's lustful gaze until he was satisfied he would appear to have evaluated the situation politely enough not to cause affront if he got in his car and left. Then he nodded to the gent and did just that.

Partway down the track to the highway, Delmont got the feeling he had exited in a different direction from which he had entered the compound. Given the scrub desert flora as far as could be seen surmounted by something that looked like ridges or trees in several different points on the compass, he had little to go on to determine whether the feeling was just some subconscious anxiety about not having added to the mine owner's satisfaction or a genuine, inner gyroscope telling him he was not on the path he had been on earlier.

Almost two hours later, Delmont Thomas stood at the end of that unpaved road, with two different ways to go, a dead battery and no bars, and nobody left to blame. Head for the hills or the alleged forest? Make the best choice you can make given the information you have. His gut said forest.

Naturally, he turned right toward the hills. It was as un-thought-out a move as turning down the track to the mine. But, the turn down to the mine had resulted in Delmont finding other human beings, something largely missing from his days recently and nonexistent in his nights.

Somewhere in his brain, Delmont knew turning right had been a good move. Not yet a time to celebrate, but a moment worth remembering as he felt more comfortable with himself than he had in weeks. He could actually feel his shoulders loosen up a bit from unloading some of the burden.

At least he did until the source of the two-stroke chainsaw noise made itself evident. Not a quarter of a mile down the road, two motorcycles approached heading for the forest, mufflers grinding out that sound that marked bikers who didn't give a shit about anyone else's rights to peace and quiet. That explained why the noise had sounded much closer than the horizon.

The bikers raised their left hands from the handlebars in that salute that indicates they think you are part of their tribe. When one is driving an eighth-generation Eldorado on a desolate highway in southeastern Oregon or northwestern Nevada, chances are bikers will assume that.

Delmont slowed down. He was curious whether the bikers might turn off to the opal mine. He kinda hoped they would. He watched the motorcycles insert themselves into the highway at the point where perspective made the narrow strip of asphalt seem to disappear. The sign of dust rising indicated they may have been seduced by the possibility of finding rainbow starlight in a rock. Before long the clamor of the machines was merely an echo reproduced by senses that also had conjured several visual mirages.

Nothing more to do but drive. The radio in the old Eldorado was stuck on a channel. Delmont took pride in checking whether a signal was broadcast at that frequency at least once a day. He couldn't remember if he had checked earlier, but thought not since there had been not much of anything to broadcast to in this stretch of road.

Instead of turning on the radio, he pushed the gas pedal down further to a point where that special V-8 engine sounded more like it enjoyed the trip. As a result, the ridge that separated this valley from the next became more defined.

Before long, the extensive hood of the Eldorado was plowing its way up the slope of the now winding road. The overcast had broken up a bit, but the land and sky were still too vaguely illuminated to determine the time. Not that it mattered much. He had nowhere to go and didn't mind when he got there.

The car reached the top of the incline and leveled off for a short while. Just as it seemed the road was starting to head back down, a pair of crows inspecting the ground around some sage took off, perhaps spooked by the oncoming presence of that once-splendid vehicle.

Crows in the dry landscape were as welcome as finding seabirds about in the ocean. They wouldn't have strayed too far from more comfortable surroundings. A town of some size must be coming. Perhaps not right away, but the black birds provided hope. Sure enough, at the far side of the next valley the road met another. The signs indicated Mr. Thomas had been travelling on Route 140 and was now in Nevada. Winnemucca was maybe an hour away at most.

Much of the remaining pressure on Delmont's shoulders dropped away thanks to that green piece of metal. Now would be a good time to see if any music might come out of that radio. He turned the knob for volume and was met with an announcer reminding all within hearing that this afternoon was the kick-off of Winnemucca's Basque festival. Things were looking up.

The first place Delmont headed to once in town was a truck stop along Interstate 80. Sure enough, that was the best spot to charge his phone, use the facilities, and decide whether he ought to eat there or check out the offerings at the festival.

He felt comfortable enough with the ladies at the counter to leave his phone for a while to charge. By chance, one recommended he ought to go to the festival while he was waiting. She assured him it was a one-of-a-kind experience. And she offered to bring his phone to him. Was that a come on? Delmont allowed the idea, but paid it no attention.

In a town of less than eight thousand residents, it was easy enough to find the festivities in the old downtown area near the bank famous for having been robbed by Butch Cassidy. Delmont found a parking spot and shuffled out of the car and down the block to see what was what. And what he saw was surprising.

Delmont was relatively certain he had seen her before. She looked like a shorter version of Allison Janney. Then again, a lot of women in places like Winnemucca looked like shorter versions of Allison Janney. It's a strange but true fact that women living in similar conditions wind up looking like one another after a while because they share the same clothes, hairdressers, make up, lighting, and life stresses. Just look at the women on Fox News.

At present, Delmont needed to decide whether to approach her or not. This was again one of those choices that had specific features. It fell into the same category as applying for jobs, submitting stories to literary magazines, and gambling. If one does not take action, the answer will always be no. That means never getting the job, never getting published, and never hitting the jackpot. That meant never picking up the woman. One must take action for there to be any real choice.

Knowledge of that fact did not make it any easier to go through with the required action. The trick came in believing there is respectability in asking even if the answer winds up being no. The honor lies in the doing, not the result.

Of course, the situation would be much easier if Delmont lubricated his confidence with alcohol. That had been the attraction of using and drinking back in the day. Everything was much easier to handle drunk or high. However, in that case, the honor would no longer lie in the doing since the doing would be supported by artifices designed to reduce the psychological challenges of doing.

Besides, Delmont Thomas was no stranger to rejection in courtship since he started abstaining from those magical substances. Sobriety never softened the blow, but being sober dampened the recoil from defeat. Actually, the uninebriated man tended to score more often with the ladies, particularly since he no longer used terms like 'score' to describe engaging a woman sufficiently that she was happy to go out with him.

Since Delmont thought so little of the future, time mattered not in deciding when a decision needed to be made. He sometimes allowed himself to visualize circumstances, such as being in a burning building or lopping off a fingertip, when decisions needed to be made quickly or face the consequences. Yet even then he could not see why promptness carried any more weight than steadfast optimism that all would work out for the best. Give time time and all that. Theoretically and philosophically, that made more sense to him than responding in a state of urgency. All the same, allowing things to work out for the best meant being rather cavalier in choosing what to do or resulted in opportunities lost.

Perhaps it depended on the importance one presumed any given decision had in the scheme of things. What was that about minor choices being made without the least scrutiny? So many impulses and trivialities needed to be dealt with. The majority were dealt with peremptorily due to the lack of importance attached to any one of them. The things that gave one pause caused the gears to begin to grind into action assessing the situation and reaching a conclusion.

Strangely enough, seeing the woman brought back a memory Delmont had of coming across the story of the crying philosopher. He couldn't recall now why Heraclitus was known for crying. He did remember the wisdom that was at the center of the ancient Greek's way of thinking. No one ever steps into the same river more than once.

Remembering that made Delmont realize it didn't matter if he had ever known her or not. At this moment, they were two different people than when they had met before, *if* they had met before. If they had known each other...what?

He figured he had another fifteen minutes to kill until his phone would be ready. Why not spend at least part of that time sidling up to the woman and making his presence known. Besides, with all that had been happening recently, being shot down attempting to escort a lady around a street festival in Winnemucca hardly seemed to be the kind of rejection that could deflate his ego any further.

Circumstances made it easier for Delmont to say something to the woman once he approached her. She seemed to be in line to purchase food from one of the vendors. No one was behind her. Before it was her turn to order he pardoned himself and asked her if she had any recommendations from the menu.

She turned to face him and he immediately knew who she was. The fast smile and embrace meant she knew him as well. Of all the places to run into each other. Then again, the festival attracted folks from around the region. It was a prized item on the calendar in a region that could bore the hell out of the dullest people. Finding her proved he was heading in the right direction after all.

Before they could say much of anything, the woman from the truck stop came running up. She looked a bit put off by the competition when she stuck her hand out with Delmont's fully charged phone. He politely accepted it and asked her to stay a minute. Then Delmont Thomas turned to Ariana Delgado's wife and wished her well. No, he might stop by sometime he told her, but the purpose of this trip was not to see them. Not this time. And with that he asked the young woman from the truck stop if she needed a ride anywhere. She said yes and that cinched the deal. Delmont was already feeling the serenity of a life set on cruise control.

They made their way through the crowd back to the Eldorado. As they approached, a crow flew directly over their heads and landed on the hood. It looked at them. They stood some distance away and watched the crow watching them. Another crow flew directly overhead and landed beside the first. One crow squawked. Both flew away. The two strangers followed the crows with their eyes until the birds disappeared, looked at each other, and got in the Eldorado. Now there was only one way to go with five bars, a full battery, and nothing to blame anyone about.

About the author:

Bear Kosik started his fourth career as a writer in June 2014. Five of his short plays premiered in NYC festivals in 2016-17 and a full-length was performed as part of NY Summerfest 2018. He has (co)authored four novels and a book on democracy that explains how he predicted Donald Trump's victory over a year before the election. His fiction, poetry, photo art, and essays have been published by Third Flatiron Press, River & South Review, Calliope, Windmill (Hofstra University), Weasel Press, opednews.com, and others. His screenplays and television scripts have garnered over fifteen laurels in competitions since 2016.

SUBMISSION
©2020 by Denise P. Kalm

Wail al-Shehri fidgeted in his first-class seat, anxious to start the mission. The day had begun badly. Some of the team had been selected for additional screening of their checked luggage and now a delay in the departure time threatened the timing of their plans. To make a forceful statement, all planes were to be hijacked at the same time. What was the hold-up? Had they aroused suspicion?

Each member had undergone the same rituals, preparing for his death as a jihadi and rebirth into Paradise, even as he believed they only had to hijack the planes. Wail had not prepared for arrest and incarceration, which would have been his fate had anyone figured out their plan. The mass hijacking would be a triumph against the Great Satan, the beginning of bigger and more audacious acts. The pilots knew the real plan; as the brother of one of the pilots, Wail knew too. Today, he would be allowed to end his earthly life as a suicider. He thrilled at the idea of being part of this war. Wail had worried as the doctors evaluated his depression, finally deciding it shouldn't stop him from contributing.

Finally, American Airlines Flight 11 took off and Wail took a few cleansing breaths, hoping to loosen his muscles. They had been trained how to act like tourists, but the growing excitement made it difficult for him to play the role. He looked at his seatmate, his brother Waleed. He looked ready to bolt into action.

"It's time."

Mohammed Atta and Waleed rose and stormed the cockpit door, brandishing utility knives. Wail and Abdulaziz al-Omari followed, forming a protective wall for the Muslim pilots. Wail unclenched his jaw. The teams had studied and rehearsed; Americans caved in quickly to hijackers' demands. The FAA dictated that pilots cede control of the plane to hijackers if asked to do so.

Wail stared out of the exit door window, watching for the target. *The passengers are like sheep*, he thought. *They believe it will all be okay for them, just a run-of-the-mill hijacking.* A short time later, the metal, hump-backed beast of Manhattan's many skyscrapers loomed ahead, too close. Flight attendants tried to calm the passengers. He glared at them, warning them not to approach the cockpit door.

The buildings neared and Wail braced for impact.

"*Allahu akbar!*" Waleed screamed as the twin towers loomed. "Today, we will be reborn in Paradise."

Wail fought off the few brave souls who tried to storm the cockpit and murmured "*insh'allah,*" giving himself up to jihad. As the plane pierced the tower, shrieks lashed at his ears. He joined them while breath remained in his lungs then the metal skin of the plane crushed his body. The smaller bones of his face gave first then pressure forced his eyes from their sockets.

"*Die already, die,*" he told his body, the excruciating pain not giving away to merciful oblivion. He felt every blast of flame in his crushed body and watched as his skin blackened. Through his screams, he tried to focus his mind on the promise of Paradise. Finally, he felt the last vestiges of life extrude through his charred lips.

Wail came to, shocked to find himself alive and his body intact, though the memory of the unbearable pain still lingered in his synapses. He opened his eyes and found himself again in a plane, this time huddled in the middle seat on a wide-body with a boarding pass clutched in his fist. LHR-JFK—he realized he was now leaving London. The date on the pass was 12/21/88. Unclasping his seatbelt, he tried to stand, but the acceleration of the plane knocked him back.

What is happening? Why am I here? Nothing in his study of the Holy Qur'an spoke of this. He had died, hadn't he? Where were the blessed virgins? Could the imams be wrong?

Wail squirmed in his seat unable to get comfortable while his questions remained unanswered. The minutes dragged. He had only the inflight magazine and a duty-free catalog to entertain him. As soon as the crew turned off the seat belt indicator light, Wail pushed his way to the aisle and headed back to the restroom. The concussion threw him to the floor as the plane exploded, then tossed his body as if it were a travel pillow. The sudden depressurization knocked many unconscious but not Wail; every sense was on high alert, his nerves shrieking. His body slammed against the overhead bins, then back to the wall. He felt the crunch of his bones each time his body hit something and he stared in horror as his shattered femur pushed through the skin of his thigh. His blood-slickened hands couldn't grab on to anything to anchor him into position.

Wail became aware that the plane was hurtling downwards. *What are the pilots doing? Why aren't they saving us?* He knew that a bomb had gone off—he could smell the Semtex. He tried to brace for the crash he knew was coming but couldn't maneuver himself back into a seat. The impact flung him upwards and he found himself impaled on a torn section of the plane's skin, the metal piercing his lungs and his heart.

Wail stared out into a frozen landscape. On this flight, he awoke after takeoff finding himself in a window seat. Fumbling in his pocket, he located this flight's boarding pass. KAL-007 to Seoul, Korea. He knew that flight, remembered hearing about it, but the details were foggy in his mind. At critical points in his life, he wondered if he hadn't abandoned teaching at an elementary school to work for Al Qaeda, would he possibly have had a life of study, perhaps a life devoted to learning about history? Then he might know what to expect. He began to believe that this flight too was doomed. Perhaps he could tell someone and save himself. The memory of the terrible pain he had experienced made him shudder. *Not again!*

But tell them what? I don't know what to warn them about.

On the last flight, had he only realized what was happening to him he might have been able to warn someone, but there hadn't been time. As he recalled now, something happened to this flight well into its journey, but he couldn't remember the details. Wail debated issuing a vague warning to the pilots, but realized it would make him look guilty or suspicious to the crew. And he had no idea what to say.

The flight reached cruising altitude and most of the passengers took the opportunity to sleep. Wail couldn't—he struggled to remember the details of this air disaster. Suddenly, he could hear a screech and saw a strange fighter jet in the distance. Too late, he remembered hearing about this air disaster. As he forced his way out of his seat, the plane began a steep ascent, the result of the missile strike. The explosion jarred open the overhead bins, but he heard only the screams of his fellow travelers and the thuds of luggage, not the missile blast. Surprised, he found himself uninjured. The plane had not broken up or exploded as he feared, but decompression sucked the air from his lungs. The aircraft descended rapidly, spiraling down. He could see a small island beneath them. He wondered where they were. Not Korea. Certainly not Korea.

The plane crashed, plunging into the ocean depths. As it broke up from the impact, he fought to find air, but quickly had to breathe in the brackish sea water, choking him, yet not choking the life out of him. Drowned passengers floated by him. The flash of light from the crash blinded him and then, all went dark. No light to find an exit. No light anywhere.

No relief. Wail found himself in a plane that reminded him of old photos of prop planes. His fellow passengers, dressed in business clothes, chatted as if at a cocktail party. The logo displayed on the bulkhead resembled that of United Airlines, but it looked different, dated. He searched his pockets for a boarding pass, he found instead an old ticket, the red carbon ink staining his hand. Today, the destination was Midway airport in Chicago. He had no memory of boarding the flight or even taking off. Looking out the window, he recognized the terrain near Las Vegas. They'd spent time there, enjoying the forbidden night life, just before the September flight. Wine, strange mixed drinks and those women! Amazing women clad only in shiny beads. Wail didn't know if the alcohol or unaccustomed desire had addled his brain more.

He looked at the emergency card; the plane was a DC-7. *Are those still flying? What year is this? Another crash? What penance am I serving and how can I earn my way to Paradise? Am I supposed to learn something first? To do something?*

In the morning light, he thought they might be nearing the Grand Canyon; he'd never seen it by daylight. Suddenly, over the wing, he saw another plane, too close. The wing of the DC-7 clipped the other plane and he watched as the wing of the other plane tore into the engine of his aircraft. He felt the unnatural, rapid descent as the plane spiraled down, the tight spiral he had seen stunt pilots do at air shows, but he knew this one would end in destruction. He didn't know what it would mean to him. The collision into a butte slammed him back into his seat and forced open many of the overhead bins. A metal briefcase shot out, crushing his teeth and breaking his nose. The sharp crack of the septum brought tears to his eyes. Again, Wail had to experience his own death, this time by immolation, an incineration that did not end in merciful death. Nor did he find Paradise.

Wail's eyes opened to another plane, another flight. Spring in 1996, flying from Miami to Atlanta. *What will go wrong on this flight? Why is this happening to me? When will it end?*

"Fire!" one passenger screamed and then all of them joined in. Smoke clouded the air and choked off the usable oxygen. While most were still fighting for their lives, the plane skidded into a swampland area, still somewhere in Florida, ending the journey by shattering as it hit bedrock. Wail found himself on the ground, still strapped into his seat. He unbelted himself and then found he couldn't walk. Both legs were broken, spiral fractures ratcheting up towards his groin, bones piercing his skin.

Maybe I have a chance this time. Maybe I will be redeemed. Painfully dragging himself along the mud, Wail maneuvered his way towards something, anything that wasn't the plane. Mangroves cut his face and hands and then he stopped himself at the edge of a river. Ignoring the murky, ink-black color of the water, he plunged his face and hands in, relishing the cool caress of the river. Spectral eyes floated on the surface a few feet away. With a scream, he tried to back away, but the mangroves embraced him tightly. The alligator slinked toward him, eyes assessing the captive prey.

Wail found himself in a cocoon seat, harnessed tightly to the padded back. His seatmate clutched her beaded bag and a copy of the Holy Qur'an, her face shrouded by a pink-checkered keffiyeh.

"Welcome to World Standard Air Flight 5, sub-orbit direct to Sydney, Australia. Please ensure your seat harness is secured, your seat is upright and your tray table and luggage safely stowed."

Another plane? Will this nightmare never end? Paranoia flooded his brain and then a single thought pierced through. *What if it is my job to save everyone on this flight? What if I need to, just one time, be a hero and keep the plane from crashing? Would I then earn my place in Paradise?* The idea took root, its branches reaching out to the heavens.

He needed information. Perhaps he could figure out how this plane would crash early enough to make a difference or to show Allah his commitment. Looking for clues, he found no boarding pass, only a cell phone, still turned on. The phone seemed huge to him—all screen—and he could see his boarding pass on the face of it. He already knew the flight number and the destination. Squinting, he read the date—January 5, 2112. No hope of figuring this out.

What if jihad still exists? What if we haven't conquered the world yet? He looked again at his seatmate. *Could it be her? They were using women more and more,* he mused.

The rush of takeoff launched the slim jet at a steep angle as it accelerated rapidly toward its cruise speed of Mach 10. The end could come now or perhaps later; he couldn't count on a quick end to his torture, but now, any time spelled opportunity.

"What sends you to Sydney?" he asked his seatmate.

"Jannah," she said, returning to her Qur'an.

Heaven? Why would she say that?

"Islam means submission, never peace," she said. "Never forget that."

The woman looked out the window then fumbled through her purse for her cell phone. Instead of shutting it down, Wail watched as she punched in a number.

Awareness dawned. He'd seen this before when he trained at Al Farouq. In panic, he tried to scream to the other passengers, pressing the *Attendant Call* button over and over. Words cramped in his throat as he saw his brother, Waleed, in the seat across the aisle. *Why is he here? What can we do?*

Time collapsed as she pressed SEND and the plane exploded, shards flaying the skin from his body and shattering his bones.

Terror ripped a scream from Wail's mouth. Waleed reached across the aisle and grabbed his arm, anger and pain raging from his eyes as he spoke, "Hell is repetition."

About the author:

Denise P. Kalm, BCC, has been reinventing herself her entire life, beginning her career in genetics, years in various roles in IT and then training as a personal/executive coach at John F. Kennedy University and as a creativity coach by Eric Maisel. Retirement is her next reinvention; she created *Retirement Savvy–Designing Your Next Great Adventure* to help others (and herself) design a retirement of their dreams. This is her fifth book. The other works are; a novel, *Lifestorm, Career Savvy–Keeping & Transforming Your Job, Tech Grief–Survive and Thrive Through Career Losses* (with Linda Donovan) and *First Job Savvy–Find a*

Job, Start Your Career all available on all major sites as paperbacks and e-books. She also writes articles, blogs and short stories.

Websites:
dpkcoaching.com
denisekalm.com

Social media accounts:
@denisekalm
Linkedin.com/in/denisekalm

THE MONSTER WITHIN
©2020 by Ronna L. Edelstein

The phone rang just as the family sat down at the table for dinner. Harry, Vera's nine-year-old brother, ignored it, preferring to twirl mounds of spaghetti around his fork. Grandma reacted with the serenity that defined her approach to life; she delicately used her fork and knife to cut a large meatball into four edible pieces. Ma, a perpetual worrier, screamed, convinced that someone had died. Only Dad had the sense to excuse himself from the table and answer the kitchen phone.

Vera, the sole family member who knew that she was the reason for the call, hung her head in shame. The tips of her light brown bangs turned dark red from dipping into the spaghetti sauce. No one at the table noticed Vera's angst—her tears diluting the sauce and her fingers ripping her white paper napkin into pieces of confetti.

Dad returned to the table, instructed everyone to continue eating, and avoided all eye contact with his daughter.

Only after the family had finished dessert—Ma's famous Jell-O pie that usually had Vera asking for "more, please," but at this gathering, barely taking a bite—and the dishes had been washed, dried, and put away, did Dad sit on one end of the couch with Ma at the other end and Vera in the middle to discuss the phone call.

"That was Miss Gardiner, your kindergarten teacher, Vera. She said that you again took a black marker and drew crosses on Ann's art work and that you 'accidentally-on-purpose' spilled your red Hawaiian Punch on Laura's white socks. Do you have anything you would like to share?"

Vera had a lot to share. She wanted to tell her parents about the monster—not the one under her bed or hidden in her closet—but the one that lived within her and made her head pound, her throat tighten, and her tummy ache. She had never met the monster, but she knew it was green—the dank green of spoiled spinach or the brownish green of dehydrated grass. Sometimes the monster lay dormant, but when it chose to use its sharp claws to gnaw at Vera's soul, it caused Vera such a profound feeling of jealousy that she lost control of her moral compass. The monster, not Vera, caused her to target Ann who, even as a five-year-old, showed promise of becoming a great artist, unlike Vera, whose paintings all consisted of stick figure people and boxes for houses. The monster goaded Vera into striking out at Laura whose white socks with lace around the ankles made Laura look like a princess and Vera feel like Cinderella before the arrival of the Fairy Godmother.

Of course, Vera could not tell any of this to Ma and Dad. As a five-year-old, she did not have the language or insight to explain herself to others. She also did not want her parents to see her as a bad seed—as some devilish person disguised as a little girl—or as an ordinary child instead of an extraordinary one who would always occupy the highest rung on the ladder of success. If she told them about the jealousy that consumed her, they would feel they had failed Vera by not giving her everything she wanted—and believed she needed. Vera remained silent, hating herself and the green monster that eroded her body, but lacking the courage and ability to confront her demon and accept herself.

The couch conversation ended with Vera promising to behave. That promise did last a few years—perhaps the monster was taking a break from its heinous acts—but by second grade, Vera was again drowning in jealousy—specifically of Harry, the sixth grader who mastered every challenge he confronted. He starred in all subjects—from science to writing, from math to woodshop; he even conquered the forward roll in gym, something the gangly Vera never managed to do. Because of his academic and overall school success, he received kudos from Ma—a woman who equated earning high grades to winning an Olympic gold medal. Although valedictorian of her high school class, Ma's immigrant parents had dismissed her scholarly accomplishments as foolishness. A housewife does not need to understand Shakespeare, they told her in Yiddish, the only language they knew. Ma had dreamed of going to college and becoming a teacher, but her parents had refused to educate a daughter, leaving Ma no other option but to enter the world of retail. Seeing her son excel and have a strong future, therefore, gave her a pride that she never experienced from her own life. She tolerated Vera as a satisfactory child who never rebelled through actions or words, but also who did not do anything that gave Ma bragging rights. Vera's monster pushed the forlorn, disgruntled child to be something more than her brother and to win Ma's approval, if not love; it motivated her to seek success, not caring if the path she traveled to glory was an immoral one.

When Vera understood that she could no longer commit abusive acts on others, she sought less physically dangerous ways to address her jealousy and need for fame. Because she liked to write—the "roses are red" types of poems and the "once upon a time/happily ever after" kinds of stories—she embarked upon a pathway of plagiarism—one that she travelled on and off throughout elementary school, high school, and college, risking her reputation and putting her in danger of expulsion. Two acts of plagiarism and the contemplation of a third, however, failed to calm Vera's jealousy; rather, they gave her a profound sense of guilt that accompanied her every day of her so far seventy-two years of existence.

Prior to his graduation into junior high, Harry had served as the editor of the Bluebird Elementary School newspaper. He worked closely with Miss Harris, a behemoth of a woman who rarely smiled at anyone. She ran the library like a captain rules a ship—no book dared to stick out on the shelf or be in the wrong alphabetical order. Similarly, she supervised the monthly newspaper, making sure that the articles were of top quality. In naming Vera's brother as the editor, it seems that she found her soulmate. He, too, valued perfection; he, too, got along better with words and the Dewey Decimal System than with people.

Every month, Vera had to present a smiling façade when teachers and classmates "oohed" and "aahed" over the latest edition of the paper. Her brother's picture often appeared in an issue; the girls gushed over this handsome young man who lacked the big lips and chinless profile Vera had inherited from her father and his family. Vera waited impatiently for Harry to graduate. Only after he was safely ensconced in a different school was third-grader Vera ready to take her first plunge into plagiarism to, hopefully, assuage the intense jealousy she felt towards Harry—and to earn Ma's praise. She would shine as the brightest star by getting something published in the paper—a poem she planned to purloin. Her inner monster curled up with excitement and anticipation.

Pretending to be a detective like Nancy Drew, her hero at the time, Vera surreptitiously studied Miss Harris's schedule to determine when the librarian left her desk. When Vera realized that Miss Harris's lunchtime coincided with her recess—a time she usually spent alone with a book—she snuck into the library. After a quick scan of the poetry books for children, she chose an anthology, more for its size that fit perfectly in her bag than for the colorful flowers on its cover or its content, and snuck the book home. That night, safely tucked away in her bedroom, Vera skimmed through the book until she found a poem that resonated with her—and sounded like the voice of a third grader. It described a little girl taking care of her dolly—washing her hair on Monday, dressing her on Tuesday, and doing other special things for her on each subsequent day of the week.

Even as a third grader, dolls played a huge role in Vera's life. She spent hours, especially on weekends, in the doll corner of the basement. Sometimes Ma joined her to do her ironing, but most of the time Vera had the place to herself. She gave each doll a turn to sleep in the one doll's bed she had, but she did tend to favor Dorothy, the brown-haired, brown-eyed doll named in honor of her beloved paternal grandma, or Ginny, the doll whose flawless face and body she dreamed of having. The glass eyes of her dolls never judged her; their painted lips never stopped smiling at her. Her doll family never made her feel invisible by forgetting to choose her for the kickball team or not searching hard enough to find her in a game of hide 'n seek. They never compared her to Linda, her locker partner who floated with confidence through the hallways; Linda's perfect teeth—even before braces—and her thick, dramatic eyebrows evoked the envy of all students. Her dolls never excluded her from sleepovers or parties, even though Vera tended to sit in the corner or disappear into the wall when she did attend a peer gathering, fearing that her dancing would advertise her clumsiness and lack of rhythm. Unlike Ma, they did not tell her she would never win a beauty contest; unlike her teachers, they did not communicate the message that, while she was okay, she would not reach the status of an academic or social leader. No matter what secrets Vera shared with her dolls—a crush on Robert, one of the taller boys in her class, or a desire to trip and embarrass Merna, the queen of the elite Stanton Girls, a neighborhood club that excluded her—they never laughed at her or criticized her. A poem about dolls, therefore, fit Vera's needs.

Seventy-two-year-old Vera often wonders what her younger self thought about as she tiptoed into the library and stole a book with the intention of plagiarizing. Did this child worry that Miss Harris would catch her and then, like an evil witch from a fairy tale, lock her up, or did the thought of glory squelch all fears? Did that little girl understand that what she was doing was wrong, or did she somehow believe that the end—fame and fulfillment—justified the means? Maybe Vera had no independent thoughts, but only responded to the urgings of her monster.

Present-day Vera sees her eight-year-old self at her desk—the same one that has traveled with her throughout life and now sits in her bedroom. She watches Vera's fingers, the nails bitten and uneven, sharpening a pencil; she observes Vera biting her tongue in concentration as she carefully printed the poem on lined school paper. After three attempts at perfection—Vera's arm had smeared the pencil markings on her first effort, and her eraser had made a slight tear in the paper on her second effort—Vera was satisfied with the results. Older Vera does not remember what that desperate child dreamed that night, but she imagines it was about Miss Harris patting her head with pride and telling her that her poem, the best she had ever seen by a Bluebird student, would be in the school paper.

The next morning, during the hustle and bustle that took over the school before the first bell rang, Vera secretly placed the book back onto the library shelf and slipped the copy of her poem into the box that said, *Submissions to school newspaper.* Much to her delight—but not to her surprise—Miss Harris loved the poem and published it. Vera basked in the praise of the entire school. Teachers who had ignored her, dismissing her as a less important person than her brother, gave her a smile and nod of approval; although Laura, Linda, and Merna complimented her, Vera gloated that their eyes contained a green cast—a sign that her monster had infected them with the jealousy that sickened Vera. Even Vera's brother praised her. "I never had a poem published," Harry admitted. Ma, whose reaction mattered most to Vera, taped the poem onto the refrigerator door; Vera found excuses to go to the kitchen for milk, juice, or a piece of fruit—just to see her poem on display. Ma also prepared Vera's favorite dessert—a lemon Jell-O pie with graham cracker crust. For a woman who believed that one could never be too thin, Ma let Vera have two pieces of pie the evening the newspaper with her poem came out—a tangible sign of her pride in her daughter. Dad, of course, kissed her forehead and smiled at her as he always did—with love, and Grandma folded a copy of the poem and gingerly placed it into the drawer that contained her crocheted handkerchiefs.

And then, a few days later while practicing cursive writing in her third grade English class, Vera's world collapsed. Miss Harris stormed into the classroom. She held a book in her left hand—Vera recognized the colorful flowers on the cover as "her" book—and a copy of the latest school newspaper in her right hand. She leaned down and, in a loud whisper that reverberated throughout the room, asked the teacher if she could speak to Vera. Vera tried to avoid her eyes, but Miss Harris's stare bore through her, causing her to rise from her seat as if she were a marionette and Miss Harris were pulling the strings. "What is the meaning of this?" Miss Harris screamed as she held up the book and the newspaper. Vera stood in silence, wishing that she could disappear and that the drops of urine she felt wetting her underpants would not intensify into a major bladder accident.

From that moment on until Vera graduated at the end of sixth grade, she was a plagiarizing pariah—the girl who had copied a poem and tainted the reputation of the newspaper and the integrity of the school. Her dishonest behavior even reached the ears of the students at the junior high—including those of her brother. For whatever reason, however, Harry never told their parents, and none of her parents' friends spoke about this to them. Vera almost wished someone had revealed her crime; by remaining silent, others condemned her to having to look at the copied poem still hanging on the refrigerator door—a daily reminder that she was a liar, a loser, and a liability who undermined the honor of her family.

Despite her minutes of fame, Vera's life of loneliness and insignificance continued; her monster refused to leave her alone. The jealousy he created within her caused Vera to stay away from the other girls during recess when they jumped rope or played jacks because she feared they would mock her inadequacies and further feed her feelings of unworthiness. Vera retreated into books, into the make-believe world she created with her dolls, and into a darkness that seemed to offer little chance of light. Vera could feel herself fading like the old family photographs of Grandma's parents and grandparents.

She did not even find it ironic that she embraced Sunday School—a weekly educational experience that emphasized the morality of her Jewish faith. Vera did not see herself in the actions of Jacob, the son of Isaac who jealousy stole the birthright from

Esau, his twin brother. When her class studied *Exodus* and Moses received the Ten Commandments from God, she did not squirm in her seat when the teacher, in his deep, god-like voice, read Commandment Eight: Thou shalt not steal. Vera did not have a visceral reaction because she did not label herself as a thief but as someone who had the misfortune of being caught—and forever denied the spotlight. Yet, she also did not love herself—not her looks, not her Brobdingnagian height compared to that of the Lilliputians who populated her world, not her jealousy of Harry and all those that made her feel "less than," and not the elusive nature of her mother's approval and love.

With the passing of time, Vera convinced herself that she would never again indulge in plagiarism because the long-term consequences had not been worth the few moments of glory. But she was wrong. Nine years later, still tormented by insecurities and never without her inner beast poking and prodding her, she again risked any bit of respect she had garnered by doing well in school by engaging in a second act of plagiarism.

When she entered Jefferson High School, her teachers saw her last name and asked, "Are you as smart as your brother, Harry?" If Vera had answered "yes," then the teachers would have expected her to perform in a way impossible for her; if she had replied "no," then the teachers would have dismissed her as "academically challenged." Therefore, Vera mumbled something unintelligible, worried that she would spend the next four years again in her brother's shadow.

Somehow, the days passed; the fall leaves became the white flakes of winter, and the snow melted, making room for the spring flowers to bloom. Harry, now in college, earned all A's, hung more framed Honor Society certificates onto his wall, and was tapped into Phi Beta Kappa. Vera joined clubs—including Future Teachers of America to please Ma—and maintained a decent grade point average, but only survived geometry, biology, and chemistry because Harry begrudgingly agreed to tutor her via phone or during the few times he came home. Ma continued to gush over "my son, the future doctor" and to see Vera as a well-behaved person with little potential or substance. Vera remained mediocre—a star only to Dad and Grandma—until senior year arrived and offered her the chance to place her name on the academic marquee.

Every year, the school had a contest for the senior students in the college track: research an artist and his/her work, and then, in a monitored, timed setting, where no notes were allowed, write a report on the artist and the art. The winner would earn a free trip to the National Art Gallery in Washington, D.C.—and get his/her picture published on the front page of *The Jeffersonian,* the school newspaper.

Vera chose to research Winslow Homer, whose paintings of the sea evoked a strong reaction from her. As a four-year-old visiting Atlantic City for the first time, she was frolicking in the ocean when a strong undertow took control of her legs and tossed her under the water. Vera remembers gasping for breath when Dad, who had been standing nearby, rescued her. That near-escape from drowning gave her a profound respect for—and deep interest in—water and its power. Thus, Homer became her focus.

Every day after school, Vera read books about Homer and typed notes on her faithful Hermes manual typewriter. However, whenever she tried to translate the notes into her own sentences and paragraphs, she became frustrated. After all, the authors who had published books on Homer and his art had done such a great job; why should she re-invent the wheel? With the encouragement of her monster, Vera copied some sentences from one source, a few paragraphs from another author, and eventually had a completed paper—a patchwork of the words of scholars.

Again, the older Vera ponders whether the high school senior Vera thought back to the poem of third grade? Did the seventeen-year-old Vera remember the look of horror and hatred on Miss Harris's face? Did she consider how getting caught as a senior would have greater consequences than being found out as a third grader—perhaps even taking away her chance to go to college?

Elderly Vera is convinced that high school Vera feverishly copying passage after passage about Homer at her desk only felt the incessant rush of jealousy—like the monstrous waves in a Homer painting—pushing her to plagiarize, to get away with something she had failed at in elementary school, and to see Ma glow as she helped her pack for the trip to D.C. Maybe Ma would even bake a Jell-O pie and pile Vera's plate with three large slices.

Then came the hard part: Could Vera memorize this lengthy paper so that she could write it without notes on the testing day? Fearing that she could not, she pretended to be ill the day of the writing contest and stayed home from school, watching soap operas on the black-and-white television in her room and reading an Agatha Christie mystery. The next day, as Vera expected, she got to do the writing after school; although a teacher who liked her was supposed to stay in the room to supervise, she said that she trusted Vera so she would be in and out doing other things. Without her knowing, therefore, Vera slid her typed paper out from her bag and began copying what she had plagiarized into the Blue Book on the desk. She almost got caught when the teacher came back into the room sooner than anticipated. Vera quickly hid the typed pages under the open Blue Book, but her odd behavior— or a piece of the typed paper—must have caught the teacher's attention. She walked towards Vera and studied her, as if she wanted to ask her a question but feared the answer she would receive. Vera kept writing—pretending she did not feel the teacher's breath heating the back of her neck. At last, the woman returned to her desk, picked something up, and again left the room. Although Vera exhaled with relief, she still feared that she would not finish the essay within the allotted time; she could only hope that what she had written would convince the judges that she had conveyed her understanding of Homer and his seascapes in an effective, award-winning way.

Vera lost the contest to Diane—the popular, pretty, perky DeeDee—whose smiling face graced the cover of *The Jeffersonian*. (Decades later, Vera heard a rumor that Diane had majored in art history in college and then become a museum curator in some large urban area.) The teacher who had had the responsibility of monitoring Vera told her that she had written well—of course she had; she had copied her essay from published works—but that not finishing made her ineligible for winning. The teacher then scrutinized Vera as she had done the afternoon of the make-up writing before adding that Diane was a worthy winner—a young woman who had proven herself to be a strong student and a decent person.

Vera trudged home that day; only her intense jealousy of Diane gave her legs the strength to move. She admitted to herself that she did not regret the entire incident—the copying, the cheating. But what she did regret was the losing—not getting fame in the school, not earning a trip to D.C., not achieving an honor that had eluded her brother, not receiving praise from Ma. Vera never paused to question her integrity as a person; she never perceived herself as a villain or criminal or someone who had done something wrong. Instead, she saw herself as the victim—as the wronged person. Vera viewed her life as a merry-go-round; no matter what she did, she never managed to grasp the brass ring. Harry and others would always be many steps ahead of her, Ma would always find fault in her, and she would always be the lonely, yearning little girl, her emotions defined by the demon that refused to leave her alone.

Since her two failed attempts to use the words of someone else to outdo her brother and garner accolades from Ma, Vera tried to eliminate jealousy from her personality. Yet, as she lay in bed at night, whether at home or in her college dormitory room, her dreams of surpassing those she viewed as superior—the Homecoming Queen, the classmate who wore a new and sparkling diamond ring on the third finger of her left hand, the girls who always had plans for the weekend—made her jealousy more profound. Vera suffered headaches, periods of laryngitis, and bouts of diarrhea; sometimes, she just wandered across the campus, lost in an all-consuming jealousy.

Then, as a college junior, Vera had to research and write an in-depth essay on the Dreyfus Affair. She checked out stacks of books from the library and began studiously reading and taking copious notes on each one. She desperately wanted to earn an "A" grade to make up for the 85% she had received on the last test—and to get an exemplary report card that would equal her brother's perfect undergraduate grades and please Ma. But as she worked, memories from third and twelfth grades filled her mind. She could hear the hissing voice of the monster encouraging her to take a shortcut by copying to ensure an excellent paper. Vera's professor would receive dozens of essays; how closely would he read any one of them? Maybe her third time as a plagiarist would be the charm.

Vera began to type, carefully copying the sentences and paragraphs from the different books piled on her desk. Then, like Scrooge in Charles Dickens' *A Christmas Carol*, visions of ghosts from the past began to haunt her. She saw the scowl on Miss Harris's face and the dismissive look in the eyes of her classmates. She saw the glowing face of Diane—the essay writer who had won the contest by following the rules. Vera knew that she did not have the energy to relive those experiences. The lasting negative consequences suddenly loomed larger than what she feared would be hollow short-term results—a victory over her medical school brother, who probably would not care, and a stamp of approval from Ma that would surely wash away with time. Not even an A+ would earn her a date to Homecoming, a circle of lifelong college friends, and a sense of worth that always lurked beyond her reach.

Vera wrote the Dreyfus essay in her own words, receiving a respectable but not outstanding grade, but also knowing that she had no repercussions to fear.

Vera, now a semi-retired educator and occasional (but always honest) writer, understands that she never plagiarized out of laziness; she never cheated because she belittled the assignment or the teacher giving it. Instead, she stole words to find an outlet for her jealousy and to overcome her feelings of inadequacy. When Vera "sinned" by plagiarizing, she forgave herself, believing that her emotional desperation justified her actions. She used plagiarism as a way to boost her self-image and enhance how others—especially Ma—saw her, not realizing how her choices continued to empower the green-eyed monster that loved to make her miserable.

Sadly, none of her plagiarizing efforts changed how she felt or how others saw her. The attendees at her fiftieth high school reunion ignored her as they had done half a century earlier, and Harry, even as a retired physician, continued to surpass her mentally and financially. When Ma died a decade ago, her mind was so foggy that she barely recognized Vera. Any achievements Vera had accumulated no longer mattered as Ma lay in her hospice bed. Vera now understands that her lifelong itch to become a star only diminished her contentment and made her pursuit of happiness a futile one.

Vera also recognizes that subduing her plagiarizing proclivities did not kill the monster within. Jealousy has remained an integral part of her. Her envy of others has caused her to highlight their faults—and to end her friendship with them. Jealousy has tainted the way she views her children and their lives; instead of appreciating what they do have, she only focuses on what they do not have—the fairy tale lives she deludes herself into thinking their peers enjoy. Vera spends hours Googling former acquaintances, feeding her jealousy by convincing herself that they live golden existences while she is doomed to a life of darkness.

Just as the serpent, jealous of God and His reign in heaven, pushed Eve to eat the forbidden apple, so did the monster of jealousy take root in Vera's soul, forcing her to play a comparison game she could never win. It slithered through her life, turning her into a plagiarist and a perpetual self-loathing, insecure woman—someone whose only happiness, albeit temporary, came from another's misfortune. Forever and always, Vera will look in the mirror and see the monster within glaring victoriously at her.

About the author:

Ronna Lynn Edelstein, who earned a Bachelor of Arts Degree from the University of Pittsburgh and a Master of Arts in Teaching degree from Northwestern University, is a part-time teacher at the University of Pittsburgh English Department's Writing Center. Her works of fiction and non-fiction have appeared in *DreamquestOne* (first place), Scribes Valley Publishing (twelve consecutive years, including first, second, and third place, as well as honorable mention), *First Line Anthology, Pulse: Voices from the Heart of Medicine* (online and print), *Seasons of Caring, The Jet Fuel Review, The Pittsburgh Post-Gazette*, and *The Washington Post*. Ronna spends her free time reading, ushering at local theatres, and taking daily naps.

COUNTING FLOWERS
©2020 by Leslie Muzingo

When I was twelve, I began going with Daddy on Saturdays to where he did landscape work in New Orleans' Garden District. He gave me light chores and taught me how to care for flowers and shrubs. I liked the work fine until I overheard his white boss-man saying some things about Daddy to someone I didn't know. What made me maddest was that my Daddy heard himself called by that bad word and did nothing about it.

I fingered the contents of my pockets to try and fiddle away my anger. My hand felt the familiar things: string, a rubber band, a few pennies, a broken compass, and some chalk. The chalk was for our neighborhood game of sidewalk tic-tac-toe but using it to get even seemed better at the time.

I shoulda known Daddy would catch me.

Daddy yanked me to my feet and held onto my shoulder with no light touch. "What are you doing?"

I raised my eyes to meet his. "Why'd you let them talk about you like that?"

"Boy, words don't mean nothing. Only deeds matter. Mr. Beaumont's been damn good to us. So, if he wants to tell his friend that I'm his yard nigger, you're going to ignore it and not draw no racist pictures on his wall."

"Racist! No, no, Daddy, the New Black Panthers are—"

"They're racist," Daddy hissed. "That group ain't nothing like the Black Panthers in my day. Now scrub that fist picture offa that wall."

Later, Daddy bought me some paper and colored pencils. "You got talent. Git a library book to teach you to use this stuff. And don't be shaming this family with no racist pictures, you understand?"

I nodded.

Eventually, I learned two things from the events of that day. I learned how to draw, and I learned that my daddy was wrong. Words do matter.

Over the next few years, I drew on paper when I could get it and on the side of our house when I couldn't. When I was sixteen Uncle Charlie gave me some old cans of paint. That gift bloomed into an arbor of red roses around our front door. Soon all the womenfolk around us were talking about my painted flowers and how they wanted some for their houses. By the time I'd graduated from high school in June of 2005, I'd put a garden on almost every home on our street.

"My son's a landscape artist! He learnt his flowers from me and look what he's done with his learning!" Daddy bragged to anyone who mentioned the splash of color on our street. He took to calling our neighborhood the "Ninth Ward Garden District."

August of 2005 was as hot as it gets in New Orleans. The afternoon sun burned over the city like a ring of fire and wrung the water out of our bodies. Television weathermen tried explaining how the humidity could be so high without a rain cloud in sight, but none of us really understood. We were dry on the inside, soaked on the outside, and our houses were more like saunas than places to call home.

There was a storm brewing in the Gulf. Most folks were glad because a hurricane meant rain and rain meant relief from the heat. Mama watched the weather reports all day, studying the predictions of where the storm would hit and when. As soon as the sun went down, she lit the old gas stove and baked like a holiday was coming.

Sister whined that she was just the right color of blackness, and would Mama quit trying to use the oven to crisp her up? It earned her a pop on the mouth. Mama wasn't playing; she had her mind fixed on getting us ready for the storm.

Baby Brother was never one to talk much, but that night he spoke out. "Mama, it ain't gonna hit us. The neighbors done said we're not even in the cone."

Mama stopped kneading the bread she was making. One flour-covered hand went to her hip, and the other she used to shake her finger at us as she spoke. Bits of dough flew, but Mama was too angry to notice. "You kids think you know so much. Who went through Camille and Fredric? Me, that's who. Who's been studying this storm ever since it got to Cuba? Me." She emphasized her words with a small stomp of her foot, which caused dustings of flour to swirl. "We won't be staying here, not for this storm. Time you three figgered out why. Now go sit in front of that television, watch the weather, and keep your mouths shut."

Our sweaty legs stuck to the black vinyl couch, but we did what Mama said—we kept our mouths shut and only spoke to one another through fear-filled eyes. Watching the news made us finally realize the size and strength of this storm.

Mama wasn't the only one getting our family prepared. As soon as he walked in the door Daddy announced, "I got the car tuned up good today. Even the air conditioning works. Get everything ready; we leave tomorrow."

The next morning Daddy said he had some errands to run. By the time he came home, we'd already gotten the bad news that the cone had shifted, and New Orleans was a possibility for a dead hit.

Everybody got in the car as fast as they could. That is, everyone but Daddy and me. I was fussing at Baby Brother to move over so I could sit by a window when Daddy said, "Junior, wait, I want to talk to you a minute."

Daddy walked several yards away from the car before handing me the car keys. "Son, it's up to you to get the family out of here."

It took a second for what Daddy was saying to really sink in. For one thing, only Daddy drove our car. Mama and I both had a license, but the car was too important to the family's survival for us to use. But once I got my mind wrapped around the idea that I would drive, that's when it hit me the reason I'd be driving.

"No," I cried. "We ain't leaving without you!"

Daddy gave me a look, and a feeling of doom pressed down on me. As if I were trying to hold onto my childhood for one last moment, I quit listening to Daddy and instead counted the houses I'd painted with flowers as far as I could see.

Daddy was looking at the ground, so he wasn't really paying attention to where I kept my focus. "We can't fit Uncle Charlie in our car, and then there's Gram and Grampa."

Red roses—one, I thought.

"Someone's got to get them to higher ground,"

Sunflowers—two. I started keeping track of them with my fingers. This wasn't time to be making no mistakes.

"...and that falls to me," Daddy continued.

Morning glories—three. I turned a little away from Daddy. I wanted to count the flowers on the walls and he was distracting me.

Daddy took my arm. "Son, pay attention."

Zinnias—four, went through my head.

"Drive the family to Dallas. You can do this," Daddy pressed on my arm. "Aunt Nessa's expecting you."

I found strength in my Daddy's eyes. I quit my counting. "Okay," I said and got behind the wheel.

Before Mama could squawk, Daddy crossed over to her side of the car. He opened the car door, yanked Mama out, and spun her into his arms. Daddy was kissing her long and deep before she could protest.

The effect on Mama was immediate. She went limp and got what Daddy called "bedroom eyes." Then Daddy helped Mama into her seat and got down next to her on one knee. I'll never forget what he said, "Woman, my love for you won't never die, and stop your fretting because I'm not gonna die neither, that I promise you here and now." He gave her one tender kiss, stood up, closed the door, and simply said, "Drive."

I hated thinking about Daddy standing there, alone in the dirt, as we drove away. To get the image out of my head, I went back to counting the flowers I'd painted on the neighbor's walls. I got as far as Angel's Trumpet, number twelve, when I came to the end of our street. I made the turn, and through the mirror, I could see Daddy standing in the same spot we'd left him.

We weren't the only ones leaving town. While most folks in our neighborhood didn't have the means to go, the rest of New Orleans packed the highways. New Orleans drivers drive fast and when they can't get moving quick enough, they yell out their windows. But not now. It was ominous, like a funeral procession honoring the death of The Big Easy.

Mama didn't say a word until we stopped for gas in Jackson. "We ain't going to Dallas. We going to Atlanta. So, you go east on 20, not west."

"But Mama, Daddy said—"

"I don't give a flip what your daddy said. I'm here and he ain't. So, when I say turn east on 20, you do it!"

Mama grumbled all the way to Atlanta that she was in charge, not Daddy, and not no kid neither. Said she wasn't gonna stay at Nessa's house, no way, no how. She had her own people, thank-you, and we'd go there.

We went to Mama's cousin Jackie's house. I called Nessa to tell her, but her phone had been disconnected.

We'd spent more'n two days driving, so we all collapsed in the spare room Jackie gave us. I musta slept more'n twelve hours. When I got up, I found everyone else crowded around the living room TV. Mama was crying.

"Mama! What's wrong?" I cried, rushing to her side. I tried to comfort her, but she brushed me off. I looked at what was on the screen. People were sitting on rooftops—crying and shivering—until they were rescued by men in helicopters. Before flying them away, the rescuers got out a can of yellow paint and marked the roof with a giant X. The X's were filled in with numbers.

"What are they marking on the roofs?" I asked. "Where is this?"

It was with an old man's eyes that Baby Brother turned to me and said. "This is New Orleans, the Lower Ninth Ward. The top numbers are the date, and the bottom ones show first how many people are inside dead and how many people were found alive."

Mama took to her bed. She kept muttering, "He promised me. He promised me."

Sister looked up, and Baby Brother and I met her gaze. With Daddy missing and Mama like this, our life in New Orleans was dead and washed out to sea. It was at that moment that we knew it was time we stopped being teenage kids and grew up.

Baby Brother and I each got jobs while Sister stayed at home to help Cousin Jackie with Mama and the house. Our jobs weren't much, but it helped put food on the table. Baby Brother couldn't do nothing but fast food work, and he had to lie about his age to even do that. As for me, I was eighteen and a man, but I wasn't a man when it came to work. I had no experience, so I worked as a day laborer. It was hard work, but I was diligent, so I'd get chosen on the next day. And the next.

It haunted me, not knowing what happened to Daddy. I'd called Nessa several times with no luck before turning to the online database; it said that more'n eighteen hundred died in New Orleans, but that number was only the bodies that were found. I'd slapped one of Cousin Jackie's boys for saying our daddy had probably been eaten by a gator, but it coulda been true. I had to know. Was Daddy still in New Orleans?

I told Mama I was leaving, but I'm not sure she heard me. She just laid in bed staring at the floral wallpaper.

Katrina had hit months before, but the drive to New Orleans was as spooky as if it'd been yesterday. Outside of Birmingham miles of giant pine trees were snapped in two. In Jackson, businesses were still boarded up. Every town I went through was either busted, broken, or drowned.

The water had receded in New Orleans, but the ground was still sloppy in the Lower Ninth Ward. Fresh spray-painted X's marked each door much like the blood that smeared the doors in the Book of Exodus. Yet this was no stain for Passover. The Destroyer had already come, and these fresh marks showed more dead had been found. A lot more dead. The number of dead in my neighborhood now far exceeded the number of those rescued.

What had happened to everyone? What about Gram, Grampa, and Uncle Charlie? What about my childhood friends, those who attended our church, and the girls I had dated? Did they escape? Or did the rising water swallow them all?

I found our street. The road was clean washed away, but I knew it was our street by the flowers painted on what was left of the houses. Seeing the number of dead painted on our neighbor's roofs, smelling the mold and rot, was too much. I sat in the mud and looked in the direction where our house once stood and cried like a baby.

Crying can clear a man's head and give him direction. Once I dried my eyes, I drove to the nearest hardware store and bought every color of spray paint they had in stock. I then went back to our street and got to work.

I painted on the remaining houses in our old neighborhood until I ran out of paint. Soon there was a fresh garden with roses, hydrangeas, azaleas, daisies, and every flower I could remember from when Daddy took me to work with him in the Garden District. On each house, I also left a colorful message. I wrote with shadowing, outlining, thin lines and bold. *Daddy we in Atlanta*, or *Come to Aunt Jackie's* was what I wrote most, but the biggest message was "You promised Mama."

Then I got in the car and started back to Atlanta.

I don't know what I expected. Maybe I wanted to be able to tell the family I tried. Maybe I wanted to paint again, something I hadn't done in months. Or maybe I wanted to find Daddy and shake him—shake him hard—for not coming with us in the first place.

I stopped at a gas station in Birmingham. The man behind the counter was too busy staring at the television hanging on the wall to pay attention to me. I looked up, and there was Daddy on the national news being interviewed by that young white-haired white reporter. A smile stretched all the way across Daddy's face and he laughed when he spoke.

"No one knew where my family had gone. But my son, my wonderful son, has been here and left me these messages!" Daddy waved toward the houses I'd painted. "Thanks to him, I know where to find them!"

That newsman praised my artwork and promised to helicopter Daddy to Atlanta.

"Here's your money," I cried to the clerk, and I threw some bills on the counter. I ran to my car, ran as fast as I'd ever run before because I wanted to be there when Daddy walked through Cousin Jackie's door.

I couldn't wait to see Mama's face when Daddy walked in the door. I couldn't wait until the family was all together again. But maybe most of all, I couldn't wait to tell Daddy that he was wrong. Sometimes words, written in the right place, do matter after all.

About the author:

Leslie Muzingo grew up in Iowa but relocated to the Deep South long ago. She was a finalist last year in the Scribes Valley *Beyond the Norm* anthology, and is thrilled to be a finalist again this year. Leslie has stories included in both the first and second *Two Sisters Writing and Publishing Anthologies* and also has been published by Darkhouse Books, Mother's Milk Books, *Pink Panther Magazine, Curating Alexandria: Welcome to Alexandria,* Literary Mama, among others. Leslie lives in Mobile, Alabama, during the winter and Prince Edward Island, Canada, in the summer. She is working on a novel.

LONE STRANGERS STRAWBERRY PATCHED
©2020 by Steve Putnam

Lady next door, my wife Dee's best friend, glass of wine in one hand, aluminum lawn recliner in the other. "Do you mind?" she asks.

No idea where she's going with this. I only know where she's coming from, the one-time dairy farm next door, barn converted to a small horse farm, not that there are enough stalls or pasture for a large herd. I nod as if I don't mind at all. She sets up a couple of feet away from the berry patch, reclines, stretches out and crosses her legs, as if she's a tourist sunning herself on a cruise ship headed for Denmark. She closes her eyes, as if to better hear clichéd birds chirping, better to feel the sun's warmth caress her face, heat up her black jodhpurs. Middle-age lady, eyes closed, she looks hot. Maybe she's praying for rain to grow bigger strawberries. How can I tell?

I pull back leaves, looking for berries, ripe, sweet, and juicy. She opens her eyes, sips red wine, takes a deep breath. She puts on a black mask, open-eyed, plain, like yesteryear's Lone Ranger used to wear on TV. Can't be sunburn protection for the rest of her face, still exposed. You can't stare into the sun, wearing a mask without sunglasses, a problem unless she moves the chair or goes back to napping. What's there to hide? Did I miss a pimple on her forehead, a blemish real, barely visible, or only imagined? I wait for a spark to trigger spontaneous conversation. Does open-eyed cover help her see light at the end of some mythical tunnel? Dark at the end of a tunnel well lit? Either way, her masquerade complements black hair, long and straight.

She reaches out, leans into the strawberry patch, picks a berry, savors it with a drawn-out kiss. If it were not for the mask, that would be bad form in a strawberry patch. She says nothing; hard to tell if she's conducting an elegant loyalty test on herself, her best friend my wife, me, or all three.

I pull back leaves, more and more leaves, picking ripe, firm fruit, untouched by marauding chipmunks.

She basks in six o'clock evening sun, as if she feels more at home near strawberries than lying in her yard by the pool, something she always does unmasked. Is she sharing solitude, a pastoral moment with a would-be farmer who works agriculturally? Not that I'm always watching, she's never out when the neighborhood boy skims the pool or landscape guy mows the lawn. An archetypal gardener, am I worthy of masked intentions?

So many to pick, hull, and freeze; so little time for talk. Lucky not much needs saying. I fill another basket, new, thin wood folded, bound at the top with staples, sun faded just enough for a vintage look. I reach for another empty. Without saying a word, she reaches out with a black mask, I'm thinking it's for me. What is it about me that she doesn't want to see? Far as I know there's not much I need to hide. It can't cover the pimple on my chin. Maybe word's gotten around that I have bedroom eyes needing to be framed for analysis. Coincidence? Am I joining Desire in a funky, secret society?

Each berry picked in a flash; each quart climaxes a string of repetitive moments. Pulling leaves back, picking, sneaking glances through a Lone Ranger mask, I feel like Mickey Mouse. So close, so far away, the moment's ripe for flirtatious conversation. Does she wonder why I'm not talking, wonder if I'm wondering why? Is it the peaceful solitude or togetherness she's looking for? Is it my turn to say something? Interrupting silence might break the spell of berry picking's magical meditation. At least we're spending quality time together.

I don't have much to say. Silence is almost deafening. I try to come up with a question that deserves a serious answer. "Any way you folks can hook me up with that old tractor?" I point to an old Ford tractor, sitting at the wood's edge, upside down seltzer can on its exhaust. Originally blue, it's painted orange, no idea why. Farm used to belong to Dee's father. Abandoned tractor went with the real estate.

"What would you ever want that tractor for?" masked lady asks. "G.A.G. says it doesn't run. It's worthless."

"Maybe fix it up, restore it."

"Why would you do that?"

I take the lady's answer as a no. Mask sweat drips into my eyes, stings, makes me blink repeatedly. Will this cover-up raccoon our foreheads white, reflect a sun framed façade of innocence? Should I worry if masquerade contradicts reality? No axes to grind, no horses to ride, woman has no reason to wear jodhpurs. It's not Halloween. I'm driven to ask the obvious. "Why the masks?"

"They make it easier to ask, 'Why the strawberries?'"

"Why not?" What else can I say? Even though the need for strawberries is not exactly a secret, it's hard to be transparent. "Of all people, never ask a farmer, why strawberries."

"Never ask a therapist what makes her tick."

"You're a therapist?"

"When you tick, I tock."

"Must be a coincidence. I was planning on being a therapist. I'm a mongrel now."

"First time I've heard a therapist call himself a mongrel."

"I'm talking therapist who builds houses. Works on robotic farm machinery, automation I don't believe in."

Lady gets out a small notebook, fancy pen, its barrel's transparent, allowing her to check the ink level, whenever she runs out of words. Never know what will happen if you end up in a strawberry patch without a fresh refill. "How do you spell *Luddite*?" she asks.

"Are you writing a book? No sarcasm, I'm just wondering why the pen and pad."

"Reclining on a recliner numbs the mind. I'm a better listener, taking notes. Luddite's spelled with two *d*s?" she asks.

"Luddite?"

"That's the word I want. You do sound like a technophobe who would assassinate a robot, given the chance. Let's move on. Dee mentioned you're a carpenter."

Awkward silence drags out, making me want to fill the silence. I do have occasional moments when I like to talk. "Not exactly a working-class hero, I'm just a farmer displaced. We plant houses on easy-access cornfield frontage, situated on roads that already exist. Cornfield's divided into building lots, sold off piece by piece, just enough to pay the tax man, get rid of the proverbial bear at the door, buy more time to stay in business. It's all about spontaneous real estate and milk prices bubbling and bursting."

"I like to think of new houses as homes for people trying to live the American Dream."

"Farmers don't care about new homeowners living some dream. Land sales save the farm temporarily, keep the economy chugging for the developers, contractors, realtors, lawyers, builders too. When things get bad, or better said, when same things get worse, another road paved displaces more cornfield, corny logic for everyone but the money people. New home buyers make love, produce offspring intended or unintended, driving demand for more houses and food grown on fertilizer-fed other-lands. Pastoral dreamland a disappearing reality, every house built displaces land to wander."

"You sound like a cynical economist. Don't take this the wrong way—I'm sure you're a luddite."

"Yeah, that's it. Reality might sound cynical; not so much for displaced farmers. There's nothing left to do but work, an old School of Agriculture tradition: Work, plant houses, laugh and joke, talk no bull."

"You make it sound better than working in the corporate world."

"I'm the new guy. Boss has fun asking if I'm a flapper or screamer. I'm always at a loss for words on that one. Afraid of heights, afraid of falling, I've never fallen far enough to know if I flap or scream."

"Your good fortune is your boss's loss."

"So, there you have it. I ride life's cycle, building stick-built houses. Boards come from forest to sawmill, lumber yard to job site. I bring lunch boxed, black coffee bottled in a Thermos. No outhouse, I pee, spraying natural fertilizer into the dirt, nature's awkward way of tipping nutritional balance, nourishing next year's lawn."

"Economy, ecology; you have a noble but dark point of view."

"Gratitude for another house roofed, windowed and sided, boss tacks a fir twig at the gable end that faces the road. It's a sacrificial Scandinavian ritual, a nod of gratitude to the gods for dead, lumbered trees, no longer taking in fresh breaths of carbon dioxide, no longer expelling oxygen into the universe. Paychecks are enough to kick the economic can of trouble down the road, keep us in business for a few weeks on the next house. Will a fir twig please the gods? Is more appreciation due for boss's tree sprigged sacrifice? It doesn't matter; remaining trees can't avenge a displaced forest. Every time we complete a job, boss always tacks a twig to a gable end. Always goes to the Chapel afterward—drink beer and watch exotic dancers, celebrate fertility, less agriculturally without a fir twig."

"Ecologist, economist, agriculturalist, you sound like a farmer who never had a chance to own a farm. You sound more fatalistic than I first imagined."

"Therapist who builds houses, works on robotic farm equipment that ultimately puts old-time farmers out-of-business."

"Working class hero; you have Dee to think about. She's worried about a woman who calls herself the girl next door."

No time to point out that a next-door woman is watching me pick strawberries while taking notes. "What about Dee?" she asks.

What are the odds? Dee's standing on the deck that overlooks a neglected lawn and weed-less garden. Wearing a black mask that looks identical to ours, she's holding a tray of shortcake biscuits. She waves. Lady in jodhpurs waves back. Three masked humans act out a fantasy well-hidden. Did my wife get into the stash early, get baked while baking? Is the lady in jodhpurs lapsing? What do I see beyond shadows?

Cover-up, the only way to hide denial. School of Agriculture psychologists claim putting on a new mask masks a previous mask; homogenizing many faces into a bland but funky composite.

No time left to ask the lady for a story. She closes her spiral notebook, gets up, folds the aluminum chair, reaches for her empty glass, turns it upside down and pauses. "Was that good for you?" she asks. Her mask makes it hard to tell if she's directing her question at me.

I pull my mask up, regain my shady identity. "Yes—definitely," I reply. "We'll have to do this again sometime."

About the author:

Steve Putnam lives in Western Massachusetts, in ancestral shadows of farmers, carpenters, and ice dealers. He has worked as a laborer, G.M. mechanic, framing carpenter. Last gig as a copier tech, he worked in schools, prisons, hospitals, and a scrap yard or two. Putnam also guest starred as copier repairman under the corporate florescence of a large life insurance company. He often paddles marathon canoes, solo or tandem with wife, Cynthia.

His non-fiction book, *Nature's Ritalin for the Marathon Mind*, was published by Upper Access. His novel *Academy of Reality*, and work-in-progress, *School of Agriculture*, both made finalist lists in the 2019 Faulkner-Wisdom Competition in New Orleans. Short fiction pieces have appeared in *Whiskey Island Magazine*, *Carbon Culture Review* online. "Seltzer Can on a Blue Tractor Painted Orange" appeared in the 2018 Scribes Valley Publishing's annual anthology. Included in the Scribes Valley 2019 anthology is "Lone Strangers Strawberry Patched," an excerpt from Putnam's novel-in-progress.

IS IT REALLY YOU?
©2020 by Lynn C. Miller

"Is it really you?" The woman in a yellow tracksuit walked up next to Ellen at the bakery counter. The fragrance of the place was buttery, hints of cinnamon and apricot wafting about. Ellen was almost too hungry to pay much attention. She turned around. No one else was nearby—the woman had to be talking to her.

"Um," Ellen adjusted her glasses. Did she know this person? The woman had a hopeful expression. "I think you might be mistaking me for someone else," Ellen blurted out. Best to be honest.

The woman stuck out a stubby hand with very short fingernails. Gardener, Ellen thought. She could just see the woman grubbing about in the dirt. Probably everything she planted came up too. "I'm Grace Norris. You look just like an old friend of mine, Betty. Betty Vasquez. Haven't seen her since she moved." Her face looked hopeful again, the smile almost too wide, her teeth square and efficient-looking.

Ellen hesitated. Wouldn't the woman, this Grace Norris, have known if an old friend moved back to town? However, the corner bakery was a cozy, friendly place—the scones looked fantastic today (raspberry, her favorite)—so why not be cordial? "I'm Ellen Alger. I'm afraid I don't know Betty." She shook the woman's hand. It was warm and fleshy.

"Well, that's a shame." Grace erupted in a wobbly laugh. "I was almost going to say it's a shame that you're not Betty. But that's not your fault, is it?"

Ellen weighed in her mind the possibilities: the scones and this woman, or no scones.... She sighed. "Do you live in this neighborhood?"

"Close by," Grace said.

The woman behind the counter handed Ellen her scone on a plate and a double latte. "Oh, thank you," Ellen said, paying her. She smiled at Grace. "Nice meeting you." She selected a table by the window and took out a thick paperback. The essay she was working on was a hard slog. She'd been looking forward to this break all morning.

She had just cracked open the book and taken one delicious bite when a voice above her said, "May I join you? You do look so like Betty. And I'm afraid my husband's out of town and I've been rattling around in the house all weekend."

Before Ellen could open her mouth, Grace sat down across from her. "I've managed to get out in the yard, cutting back the bulbs in the back, you know how dense the iris gets, but the rain today kind of put an end to that."

Ellen shut her book. It was a Patricia Highsmith. The mysterious British man in Tunisia had just pulled out his gun. "You garden?" she asked politely.

"Do I garden? Oh my, yes!" Grace's voice rose eagerly. "Do you like gardens? I don't mean to brag but I have one of the most spectacular English gardens around here. Profusions of flowers."

"Well, yes, of course, I do like gardens." Ellen heard her own voice with dismay. What was she saying?

Grace sipped her coffee, which looked to be mostly milk. "Then you must come and see mine! Really. It's only four blocks away, you know that really tall and narrow house at the end of Pine?"

Ellen licked a tiny morsel of raspberry from her lip. She felt cold all of a sudden. There was a house on Pine that had terrified her as a child. It was the kind of house that appeared in a Gothic tale, set way back from the street, a seeming apparition anchoring the 19th century in the present.

She looked at her watch. "I don't have a lot of time today," Ellen began, again wondering what she was doing leaving the door open to go anywhere with this...this *strange* stranger.

Grace waved her hand in the air. "Oh, no problem. It's a three-minute walk. I'd love to show you."

Grace was already on her feet, reaching for her coffee cup and draining it. She beamed down at Ellen. "I'd be honored for you to come over. Just for a minute."

Ellen nodded. She took a big swallow of her coffee and looked longingly at her plate. She'd devoured most of her scone in a rash of nerves. There was something about this woman...maybe she *had* met her?

"Well, I can spare forty-five minutes," Ellen said. She had to put some kind of fence around this event. "I have a deadline today..." She sounded apologetic to her own ears; what on earth was wrong with her? This Grace Norris arrived and turned a perfectly capable thirty-nine-year-old woman into a floundering nitwit.

Out on the street, a light rain had begun.

"I just happen to have this with me," Grace said, unfurling the largest umbrella Ellen had ever seen. It completely enveloped the two of them. "Bought this on my last trip to London. Can you imagine, silly me, traveling to Britain with no umbrella?"

Ellen thought frantically of a response. Should she tell Grace about her own trip to London? Should she compliment her on the umbrella? How ridiculous—it was a hideous blue and white affair. "I think the only time I was there it was sunny every day," she said in a feeble voice.

"Well, then, I hope you spent the good weather at Kew Gardens," Grace spoke briskly. "The world's greatest botanic garden. I could just live there. Sometimes when Roger is boring me to death, I think what if I just fly to London and volunteer at those gardens?"

Roger. Roger Norris, the name hit Ellen like getting coshed on the head by a crowbar. That was the man who'd lived in the spooky house on Pine when she was a kid. He was kind of a Boo Radley type, haunting the place. How old was Grace anyhow?

"Tell me this," Ellen said. "I remember that Roger's family used to own a house on Pine Street when I was growing up. Didn't they? Right at the top of that little rise...."

"That's the one," Grace said with excitement. "Maybe that's how I know you!"

"Well, that was twenty-five years ago or more..." Ellen began.

"Roger's family has owned it forever!" Grace leaned even closer toward Ellen, although the umbrella already made for close quarters around them. "He is, of course, some years older than I am."

Ellen frantically calculated how old· Roger could be. She thought he was maybe forty when she was nine; that made him about seventy now. Grace didn't look a day over fifty. The Roger she was thinking of had always seemed old. But of course, to a nine-year-old, everyone over twenty was ancient. Still. Ellen shivered as a fat raindrop hit the knee of her jeans and spread a chill along her entire leg.

Ellen walked with the woman down the street and onto Main. She remembered this street from when she'd lived in this neighborhood twenty years ago. Main Street had mom-and-pop shops that, if they were shoes, had aimed to be polished pumps but were now sadly worn down at the heels. A 1950s dowdiness prevailed, as if covered by a patina of dust that took even bright sunshine down a notch.

As soon as you turned off onto Pine Street, though, you entered another world. It was a tiny tributary leading to a dead end; reality seemed to vanish behind you.

Ellen thought longingly of the last bite of scone and the perfectly prepared latte she'd left behind at the coffee shop, accompaniments to a long-awaited book. Why had she let this woman, Grace Norris, convince her that she had to see her garden? Ellen was not fond of gardens in general.

The street sloped upward and with each step the houses grew grander and older, their details sharp in the afternoon light—wrap-around porches, mansard roofs, tiny cupolas perched like silos on the roofs, and front doors with ornate stone-framed sidelights and transoms. The houses were so large that they insulated the inhabitants from any activity on the street. Ellen remembered trying to trick or treat on this street with her brother. No one had answered the door. In fact, at each house where they'd knocked the lights had gone out.

They were trudging up the slight hill on Pine Street now. And there, ahead of them, was the house. It was high and spiky looking, painted a kind of beigey olive green, sort of like army fatigues. The windows were long and narrow too, about the size of coffins, she'd always thought. How big was that anyway, like seven feet by three feet? Ellen slowed her steps. She looked at her watch. Only five minutes had passed. She felt like running away from this claustrophobic umbrella and crying "Help! Help!" Her legs felt heavy and exhausted, as if her coffee had been drugged. How could she run anywhere?

Still, she stepped away from the umbrella and turned to face Grace. "I'm afraid I'm not feeling very well," Ellen said. "I'd love to see your garden. Another day maybe."

Grace appeared not to hear her. "Here we are," she said cheerily.

Ellen took in the house's four stories. A fire escape ran up on the left side but only to the second story. From a third story window a white face stared down at her and then vanished. Had the person winked?

"Um, wasn't your husband famous for his roses? I seem to remember that from when I was a kid."

"Oh, goodness sakes, yes. I used to say 'Roger, you don't have ten fingers but ten green thumbs.'" Grace beamed and Emily managed a tiny smile. How could she get out of this? But she was curious about the face at the window.

"Who lives here now?" Ellen asked boldly.

"Well, you know Roger passed on—he was twenty years older than me—I was lucky I had him for twenty years. So, it's just me now."

"I must have misunderstood. I thought you'd said earlier that he was out of town."

Grace looked stricken. "Did I? I'm still not used to him being gone. Sometimes I forget when I'm talking about him...I...." She wiped a tear from her eyes.

"I'm so sorry." Ellen said hastily.

As Grace touched a tissue to her face, Ellen studied the third-floor window. Was Mrs. Norris keeping a hostage in the house? A grandchild who had been abandoned? Ellen seemed to remember the Norrises had two children: the son had died in one of those freak accidents on the playing field—his heart had just stopped, and the daughter was named something like Susan, Suzette, Sigrid. Did she dare ask about her?

They walked along a cracked brick walkway from the street and through a wrought iron black gate that creaked as if it had never been used. The house glowered above them, a dowager without a sense of humor.

The drizzle had stopped, but the gloomy sky and the house cast a monochrome pall over Ellen. Yet in a few more steps they reached the back where a riot of color flooded the yard, almost knocking Ellen over with its brilliance. The garden seemed like a lost paradise, everything bigger and plumper and brighter than Ellen had seen before. Ellen wondered if the gray sky made the blooms pop, like a red rose against a neutral background.

She leaned forward to touch a begonia, flame red with green leaves arcing away from the flowers. "Is it real?" Ellen asked.

Grace's laughter was high and light, all tears seemingly forgotten. "Of course. If you see it, it's real."

"Has this always been here?" Ellen took in the huge yard, segmented into wedges—each color had its own area, she realized—and arranged in a wheel around a tiered fountain, grand in the Roman way, with several streams spouting into the air. A plump sculpture of Cupid stood in its center.

The odd thing was that it was September and the nights were getting cool, downright cold. But here in the garden the air felt fragrant and warm. A wrought-iron fence circled the area as if cordoning off the bounteous growth from the drab slabs of the house's walls. Ellen eased herself down onto a gray stone bench.

From where she sat, she didn't see the gate they'd gone through, only the fence. She wondered if it was possible to exit this place. But with honeybees buzzing, the fountain murmuring, the flowers seeming to flare open the more she looked at them, Ellen found that she didn't care.

"Ah, you're starting to relax I see," Grace said. "Time is very over-rated as a concept and certainly as a way to rule your life, I find."

Ellen felt stuporous in the heat—the temperature seemed to be increasing.

"Let me get you something cool to drink," Grace said and disappeared.

As soon as she left the enclosure—and oh, Ellen wished she'd seen how Grace had maneuvered out of the garden—a child stepped out from behind the sculpture in the fountain.

"Were you looking at us from the window?" Ellen asked.

The child, with beautiful mocha skin and bright brown eyes, nodded.

"Do you live here?" Ellen noticed that the child's clothes were antique, a white broadcloth shirt tucked into velvet breeches and black shoes with buckles.

"Sometimes," the child said—a boy, Ellen decided even though the long curly hair and full lips seemed at odds with the clothes.

"Only sometimes?" Ellen, light-headed in the heat, felt a prickle of fear. The child put a hand on her shoulder; his fingers were cold and his touch delicious. The desire to stand up and leave the garden leeched out of her.

"Here you are!" Grace bustled out from the house and handed Ellen a glass of something brown. Tea?

At the sight of Grace, the child hid behind a bank of hollyhocks, their red and pink blooms waving over his head. Ellen had a moment's fear that the other woman would discover him. Grace, in fact, held her head up in the air, motionless, the way a dog might do, as if sensing a change in the air.

"So, you live here alone?" Ellen asked nervously, sipping the liquid that tasted both minty and bitter.

Grace cocked her head and as she did, her face transformed from its genial mask into something withered and sad. Ellen put the glass she'd been drinking from on the ground and stood up.

"I have to go now," Ellen said, again seeing the garden gate they'd come through, but very far away, like the opposite goal line on a football field. Along with the wooziness she'd felt earlier came a fierce headache.

Grace smiled a sad smile. "But I'd like you to meet Roger. And, oh, my son is here today—Bertie."

"But Roger is gone you said. He passed away. Didn't he?"

Grace reached out her hand and Ellen took a step back. Behind Grace, the young boy shook his head vigorously from side to side. Unsaid words— *Caution! No! Get away!* –seemed to fall from him like sparks.

The pure elixir of loneliness washed over Ellen. She longed to fall on her knees. Tears filled her eyes and she turned to run toward the gate, which telescoped away from her and shrank to a tiny thing.

Ellen's head was very heavy. She struggled to raise it. She blinked away the tears. The smell of fresh bread wafted toward her. She sniffed and looked around. She sat at a small table, its tile top cool to the touch. On it was her book, which had fallen shut. Her coffee sat in front of her, the milk's foam flat and dispersed. Next to it was an empty plate, white, with a few flakes of pastry straying across its surface.

She checked her watch to find that only a half hour had passed. That time now felt infinitely precious and irreplaceable. She'd come to the café because she hadn't been able to write. Something was waiting for her, she'd hoped, just beyond the next line of type.

The brilliant red begonias filled her mind. Luscious, promiscuous in their redness. The garden hovered just out of view but at the edge of her mind's eye. Its richness. Its promise.

At the counter, a pleasant-looking woman turned to the person behind her: "Is it really you?"

About the author:

Lynn C. Miller's fourth novel *The Unmasking* appears in fall 2020 from the University of New Mexico Press. *The Day After Death*, her previous novel, was named a 2017 Lambda Literary Award finalist. Short plays and stories have appeared in *North Dakota Quarterly*, *Hawaii Review*, *Phoebe*, *Text and Performance Quarterly*, *The MacGuffin*, *Apple Valley Review*, and *Chautauqua Journal*. She's been nominated for a Pushcart Prize. She taught writing and performance at USC and the University of Texas at Austin. Co-author of *Find Your Story, Write Your Memoir* and editor of the literary journal *bosque*. She lives in Albuquerque.

Website: lynncmiller.com

THE PROFESSOR
©2020 by Anna-Claire McGrath

On Tuesday the Professor and I watch *Little Dorrit* naked. The Professor is a Dickens scholar, and he assures me that this is the best way to experience *Little Dorrit*.

"The novel is crap," he tells me, his arm around my belly. "This way it's at least interesting."

The Professor interjects the movie with his commentary, explaining the ways it reflects or deviates from the source material.

"Well, this is an interesting development," he says when it's implied that two of the female characters are gay. "But not entirely unwarranted."

He wants to know whether I, as someone who dates both men and women, feel that this representation is helpful.

I move my hand to his crotch.

"Well, that's an interesting development too."

The Professor is younger than most professors. In fact, he is only in his postdoc. He insists that he is not that much older than me, only nine years, and that I should call him by his first name, but I refuse. I like that he is my professor. He has sandy blond hair and a thick beard, which I'm sure he grew to make himself look older. When he teaches my class, I can tell that all of the girls want to sleep with him. But only one does.

When *Little Dorrit* ends, we are both drunk on very cheap red wine.

"I wish I could afford better wine," he says.

"Truly a cheap date."

He rolls his eyes.

The Professor is working on a piece about queer subtext in

Great Expectations. The title of his paper is *THE POWER OF POWERLESSNESS: MISS HAVISHAM AS FEMINIST ICON.* He has been working on it for three years. He wants to know my opinion as a woman, because he's worried it's not his paper to write, but then he really loves Miss Havisham and thinks people should respect her more. I tell him I have to go home.

On the bus I receive a text from my roommate, Annie. She wants to know if we can have a party this weekend. I tell her sure and then listen to Tom Petty. I have this habit when I am feeling anxious of listening to the song "Free Fallin'" on repeat. I think it's probably OCD. I listen to it over and over again until I feel calm. Then I count the number of times I've listened to it and multiply it by 50 and write that number on the notes app on my phone. On the list it reads:

250
150
850
2300
4050
3900
60000

I read it back from time to time as a method of calming myself. I don't know. It's probably insane.

When I get back to my apartment the Professor calls me.

"I miss you," he says in a whisper.

"Get over it," I tell him, and hang up the phone.

Annie is watching cartoons on the couch stoned. She giggles at me when I walk in.

"Were you at the *li*-berry?"

I nod.

"Stop studying so hard, loser. Get a boyfriend."

Then she laughs again.

She's usually nice when she's sober but weed makes her cruel. I think she's actually so nice when she's sober that she needs the weed as a release. If I were as tightly wound as Annie, I'd be in rehab.

That night I listen to an audiobook of *The Lion, The Witch and the Wardrobe* to fall asleep. My dad used to read it to us as kids, and I listen to it now that he's dead to be close to him. I remember him lying on the floor between my brother's and my room doing an Irish accent for Mr. Tumnus the faun. The actor on the audiobook can actually do accents, but it isn't the same as listening to my dad read it. I wish I had a recording of that, but of course none exists. Instead I have videos of him in the hospital, with tubes sticking out his nose, looking nothing like that young man on the carpet doing accents.

"You've been pretty quiet, Georgia," the Professor says to me in class the next day. "What did you think of *Oliver Twist*?"

I give him a thumbs down and stick out my tongue.

"Georgia is really trying hard to get an A in this class," he says to everyone. "She's really giving it her all."

I sigh and put my head down on the table.

A girl with perfect hair and teeth, who I think is named Jane, starts talking about the influence of fairy tales on Dickens. It's extremely boring and I stop paying attention immediately.

After class the Professor asks me to wait behind.

"You know, just because...I can still fail you. I don't want to do it, but I can."

The Professor does not have the nerve to fail me. I tell him so.

"The thing is, you understand literature better than anyone here. Better than Jane for sure."

"I'm waiting for my moment. I'm going to surprise everyone with my insight on the last day so they won't know what hit them."

I start to walk away and he grabs my elbow.

"You have a mind I have never seen before, Georgia. It's hypnotic. And I just don't want to see you not be all you can be."

He goes back to his stack of papers and picks out a packet.

"These are some grad schools to think about applying to," he continues. "I think you ought to consider giving it some serious thought."

I stick out my tongue again, but I take the papers.

In the hallway Jane is waiting to talk to the Professor. I can tell from her eager beaver stance that she has worked on something she considers quite profound to tell him about *Oliver Twist*. I can see her pupils dilate as he walks out.

My mom calls me as I walk home but I don't pick up. Instead I call Annie and ask her what she needs for the party Saturday. It is easier to plan a party than to plan the rest of my life, which is what my mom would be asking. She's just like the Professor, in that she likes to criticize me and claim it is just because she sees me squandering my potential. But what she and the Professor don't realize is that this is the best version of me, this is all I'm going to become.

Annie says she needs me to invite people, and I remind her that she is my only friend. Annie claims this is not true, and reminds me of Beth from my World Civ class. I haven't talked to Beth in two months. I tell Annie I will invite Beth.

When my father died, I had to take two weeks off from class. When I came back, the Professor asked me to come into office hours. He told me he was sorry, and that he was always there if I needed to talk. There was something cute about his enthusiasm to be kind, and so I asked him if he would grab coffee. But I didn't talk to him about my dad. I asked him questions about himself and he looked embarrassed. When we were saying goodbye, I kissed him. He sent me a five-page email apologizing the next day. I walked into his office hours that day and shut the door behind me. There was no more apologizing after that.

I listen to "Free Fallin'" as I walk home. Then I write the number in the notes app of my phone: 1350.

Annie is stoned again when I get home so I work on a paper I have to write this week about a Philip Roth novella called *The Breast*. It's about a man who wakes up as a giant breast. I'm completely serious. My professor—another man, not the

Professor—claims that it is a metaphor. He will not tell me what it is a metaphor for.

I text the Professor: *Philip Roth: Y / N?*

He texts me back, *Speaking on behalf of the Jewish community, I can say with authority that Philip Roth is both a Y and an N.*

He doesn't know how to text.

Annie knocks on my door.

"You've been very reclusive, lately," she says to me, musingly. "Are you starting a career as a spy?"

I shake my head.

"Do you miss your dad? You know you can talk to me if you miss your dad."

I squint my eyes.

"Is everything alright?" I ask her.

She flops into the room, Kermit the Frog style, laying on my bed.

"I really want this party to be perfect," she moans. "I invited this guy."

"Oh, *that* guy," I joke.

"I met him at that card store downtown. He was buying a bereavement card for his friend's goldfish. I have to marry him."

Annie squirms back and forth on the bed, and I try to comfort her. Pretty soon we're not talking about this guy at all, who I think is just a focal point for her anxiety about finishing college, but instead talking about the last few years, and everything we missed out on.

"Do you think there are people leaving," she asks me, "who are like, 'This was the best time of my life?'"

"Assholes," I tell her. "Total assholes."

The next afternoon the Professor and I are at Target. We go to the Target that is far out of town because we don't want people seeing us together. He apologizes about this constantly, and I try to tell him that it is no big deal.

"It's not about it being inappropriate," I tell him. "It's that I'm too pretty for you."

I insist that we walk through the toy section. There's a Batman mask that if you put on your face will distort your voice. I tell him I think he should get it and use it for lectures. It would be hilarious, I say.

"There are things beyond hilarious," he tells me, and he puts the mask back.

I look up at him, and I see that he is hurt. I wish I could say something to him to make him feel less hurt. But I don't know how to say anything serious. That's not our rapport.

"It would be better if there was a Dickens mask anyway," I say. "To make you sound British and formal."

"Ha ha," he replies, in a way that is the opposite of laughing.

We buy him some Command strips that he needs, and we buy me the alcohol I need for this party. I find a journal that says, *EVERYTHING IS AWFUL SO KEEP SMILING*. I find it comforting, and I almost buy it. But then I'm embarrassed for him to see me like it.

In his car driving back we listen to Natalie Imbruglia singing "Torn." He told me once that he has a crush on her. He thinks she still looks good now, even older.

"I don't get it," I tell him. "If you're cold and you're ashamed, why are you lying naked on the floor? Put on a sweater."

He sighs and turns left.

"So funny today," he replies.

"So funny all days."

He parks the car in front of my house but doesn't let me get out.

"I thought when we started doing this, that there was maybe a way that I wouldn't be some creepy guy preying on a young woman who needed help. I thought maybe because you're...whatever you are, that it would be a choice you were making. But it isn't and I'm hurting you. I see that now."

In my eye I can feel a tear forming. There is a little thought at the back of my head that I am the reason for every problem in the world, from global warming to self-check-out lines at grocery stores. Instead of letting the tear fall out, I shrug.

"Forget it then."

I go inside, lay on my bed, listen to "Free Fallin'" and cry. Annie isn't home so it's only the rest of the building I worry hearing me wailing. I always think if I were in a situation where I heard hysterical sobbing from another apartment in my building, I would go check on them. But no one ever checks on strangers. That's one of the things they don't tell you about adult life.

My mom calls and I'm so sad that I answer.

"Honey, are you alright?" she asks when she hears my voice.

"I'm spiraling."

"We're all spiraling, honey. Did I tell you what your brother told me last night?"

I tell her no.

"He broke up with Monica. Monica! The only chance I had that any of you would not die alone."

"I have to get off the phone."

She makes a noise with her tongue that she used to make when my father and I would make jokes and exclude her and my brother.

"No one wants to talk to me anymore. It's bad enough in this big house all by myself."

"I'm feeling sick."

I am in fact feeling sick. I go to the bathroom and vomit. While I'm lying on the floor there, Annie comes home.

"He texted me!" she exclaims.

She sees me lying on the floor, hand on my stomach. It looks like she is thinking about saying something, and then she doesn't.

"He's coming to the party and he's so excited. Did you invite your friend Beth?"

I shake my head.

"You really should invite Beth," she continues, "so you have someone to talk to. Is she gay? You could date her."

I shake my head again.

"Too bad. You look like hell anyway."

And with that she goes into her room and closes the door.

Lying on the floor, I think of a time my brother told me on the phone I hadn't done enough to take care of my dad. I called the Professor, and he picked me up in his car. He put a hand on mine, and he didn't say anything. We didn't do anything sexual. We just sat there in the car with his hand on mine, and me crying. And then I walked out of the car, and he texted me to check in that I was doing okay.

When I start to feel better, I go back to the room and look at my cell phone. I look up the Professor's Facebook page. We're not friends, because it wouldn't be appropriate, but I can still see some things with the limited view. He is so unattractive. Premature gray hair. Gray eyes. Messy, unruly beard. And yet he is all I want. He is both the ugliest and hottest guy I have ever seen.

I send him a text:

Know you are thinking you don't want to see me right now, but I really could use someone to talk to. Would you mind if I called?"

The dot bubbles form that he's texting me back. It lasts an eternity.

Not a good idea

I go back to work on the Philip Roth paper. Maybe things would have been better if instead of sleeping with the Professor, I had slept with Philip Roth. If Philip Roth dumped you, you wouldn't feel like you had your insides pulled out one by one by infected tweezers. If Philip Roth dumped you, you'd be like, "I'm better off."

I listen to *The Lion, The Witch and the Wardrobe* to fall asleep. I'm at the part where Edmund decides to betray his entire family for Turkish Delights. I've had Turkish Delights one time, and I don't think I would betray even Annie for them. I would maybe betray my brother not to eat Turkish Delights ever again, but that's not really a risk I'm facing. I wonder if there is some kind of magic tradeoff wherein I could stop eating a certain food and my dad would still be alive. I don't know of any tradeoffs like that though.

There is a career fair for English majors at school the next day. When I first heard this, I laughed. It's like having a safe sex talk with the Christian fraternity. Completely irrelevant. I'm not going to go, but then I'm walking past and I hear the Professor inside. I look in and he's chatting with Professor Carrington, the tall, blond, Jane Austen professor, and she's giving a full-throated laugh that I can guarantee whatever he said does not deserve. So, I wander in and I pointedly pick up a brochure from right by where he's standing.

"Georgia," says Professor Carrington. "You're interested in the Navy?"

I look down. That's apparently the brochure I've picked up.

"Oh yeah. I love boats."

The Professor looks me up and down. He is sad.

"I expected you to go to grad school," Professor Carrington says. "You have such a great mind for theory."

I shake my head.

"I'm over theory," I tell her. "I'm all about action now. Nautical action."

She gives me a half-smile as if she's not sure if I'm making a joke.

"Georgia has a deep sense of irony," the Professor tells her. "Sometimes it's hard for her to see her way out of it."

Professor Carrington is confused.

"Well, good luck with it," she tells me. "I'm sure the Navy would be thrilled to have you."

As I walk away, I check that Professor Carrington isn't looking and I squeeze the Professor's ass. He looks mortified.

There must be a way, I reason, to convince him that I'm not a complete waste of space. There's somewhere in me, I think, a girl he was once very attracted to. I try to imagine talking to that girl to see if she'll give me any advice. But I can't get her to speak. Her mouth is sewn shut.

The party is tomorrow and Annie has gone from obsessed to

stalker with this guy. She has done an extensive amount of Googling, and knows the occupations of his last three girlfriends.

"We have to impress him," she tells me. "Did you invite Beth by the way?"

I shake my head.

"You know it's just going to be a lot of my friends. If you invite Beth, it'll be better. I promise."

At that point, I'm exhausted. So, I send Beth a Facebook message asking her if she wants to come. She responds immediately that she would love to.

"I'm having a horrible week," she confesses. "This will make it better."

The day of the party I don't leave the house all day. I blast "Free Fallin'" and don't care what Annie thinks. I keep looking at the limited profile of the Professor, wondering if I could get away with texting him. I know I can't. So, I just keep looking, praying to Tom Petty that *he* will text *me*.

I don't make any effort for the guests. I wear some purple harem pants I like, and put on a minimal amount of bronzer. I brush my hair maybe three times, and decide it's fine. All of Annie's friends start to arrive, and they have a ball. They laugh hysterically at each other, and I wonder if any of them actually like each other, and decide it would be impossible. I think about what I could say strategically to force them all to admit their deep hatred, what secret I could uncover that would make the group explode, but I'm too depressed to hurt anyone. So, I sit on the couch and watch them laugh and laugh. Finally, Beth shows up.

She is wearing a dress with yellow flowers, and I think of Annie's question about whether I could date her. I'm pretty sure Beth is straight, but it wouldn't hurt to find out. She sits down next to me.

"Did I tell you that I had the worst fucking week?" she asks.

I nod.

She starts telling me all about it, and it really does sound pretty terrible. Her roommate puked in her bedroom, her cat is sick, her mom is insisting she move back home when she graduates.

"Do you want to get some air?" I ask.

We sit on the porch, and I watch the gap between her teeth as she continues to complain about her day. Maybe the Professor is not the be all, end all, of my life. I wonder what Beth would be like as a lover. Gentle, I imagine, she would let you do whatever you wanted. But surely, the Professor was gentle. Surely, he was kind.

"You're a good friend for letting me unload like this to you," she says. "After we haven't talked for so long."

"World Civ is one of those experiences that bonds you for life," I reply. "Like 'Nam."

She laughs.

"You're so funny. I forgot that you're funny."

I place my hand on her knee. She looks at me, confused.

"I'm so glad you came," I tell her.

I lean in to kiss her. She pulls back.

"I'm sorry. I'm—"

I nod.

"So sorry. Momentary impulse."

When I look up, I can see the Professor over her shoulder standing on the sidewalk. At first, I'm convinced this is in my mind's eye because I have been thinking about him, the whole time kissing Beth. But then I realize that it is *actually* him. I pull away and start walking towards him.

"It's not—I don't want you to think—"

Beth stands up behind me.

"I should go."

"Please stay," I tell her. "This will be done in a second."

"It'll be done now," he interjects. "You're failing my class."

"He's your...*professor?*" Beth asks.

Annie walks out. The bereavement card guy is hanging on her waist. They're both drunk.

"Oh my god, it's Georgia's secret boyfriend!"

Beth looks like she might puke.

"I thought this was her professor?"

"He's both. They think no one knows but *everyone* knows."

The bereavement card guy gives a thumbs up.

"Wicked," he says.

"This is great," says the Professor.

The voice that I'm responsible for AIDS in Africa and wildfires in Latin America comes back to me again. It is so loud that I can't hear anything but that. I start to shake first a little, then a lot. And then the voice becomes Tom Petty, and I can only hear "Free Fallin'" over and over again in my head. I realize I'm on the ground and that I'm humming it.

I look up and I see Annie, bereavement guy, Beth and the Professor all looking down at me. Suddenly it's like everyone's talking at once, but I look around me and no one is talking at all. I hear "Free Fallin'" but it sounds like it's backwards, through a straw. Beth is still looking confused, Annie is laughing, bereavement guy looks like he might be hungry, and the Professor is just standing there, staring and staring. I feel like I can't breathe. I'm still hearing "Free Fallin'." I stop being able to think.

The next moment I remember, I'm in the hospital and the Professor is asleep in a chair next to me. He is holding a balloon that says, *Congratulations on the baby!*

"Someone had a baby?" I ask.

He wakes up. He looks so young when he's just waking up. I remember that he's not that much older than me. I want to hold him.

"This was the only balloon they had left. There was no balloon that said, 'Congratulations on your psychotic break.'"

"I'm sorry," I tell him.

"I know."

He places his hand on mine.

"What am I gonna do about you?" he asks.

I shrug.

"Always with the shrug."

"I'm an idiot, Samuel," I tell him.

"Yes," he tells me. "Your mom is outside."

"Please tell her to leave."

"Okay."

After he talks to her, he just sits there while I lay in bed, with his hand on mine. It's a strange feeling, like the most sincere thing he can do is just hold my hand. I'm not thinking about anything but holding his hand when he pulls a book out of his pocket. It's *The Lion, the Witch and the Wardrobe*.

He reads it and he does all the voices.

About the author:

Anna-Claire McGrath is a second-year MFA student at Virginia Commonwealth University. Her flash fiction has been published in *no. 2 magazine* and *Dear Damsels*. This is her first full-length story publication.

Made in the USA
Middletown, DE
04 July 2020